RACING

by

J.SPICER PARR

PublishAmerica
Baltimore

First printing

All characters appearing in this work are fictitious. Any resemblance to real persons, living or dead, is purely coincidental.

ISBN: 1-4241-1743-7
PUBLISHED BY PUBLISHAMERICA, LLLP
www.publishamerica.com
Baltimore

Printed in the United States of America

RACING

"As they turn for home it's Crystalyte in front with Jail House Cat right there, followed by Speckspal," the track announcer, barked into the microphone, as he built his momentum for another exciting finish at Cajun Downs. With less than a sixteenth of a mile to go its still Crystalyte, by half a length, here come's Coleschance, on the outside with a late charge!

It was at that precise moment, that sixteen year old Joe Leblanc, knew in his heart, that he was going to win his very first recognized horse race as he coaxed his mount to the lead. "C'mon Cole, you can do it, I know you can!" He was telling the five year old gelding as he stretched out in hand riding fashion, his urging, perfectly matched to the song, I'm winning, I'm winning, as the announcer, called the finish. "At the wire it's all Coleschance with apprentice Joseph Leblanc, in the saddle!"

Joe, hadn't heard a word of it, his mind was turning gears as he stood up in the saddle to start the pulling up or slowing down, of his mount as he sailed around the club house turn. After coming to a halt, Joe, turned the horse around and started back towards the winners circle thinking, "Wow, this is all I'll ever want to do, win races." In the years to come Tee-Joe Leblanc, as he was better known did win races, and lots of them. Some of the most prestigious races in the nation. He had become yet another Cajun rider that took the industry by storm. At one time, he was the most sought after jockey, in the sport. It hadn't lasted as long as he would have liked for it to. For along the way, he had also become one of the sports greatest disappointments.

Joe, had been born Joseph Greaden Leblanc, at the Orleans Parish Hospital, in New Orleans, Louisiana. The year was nineteen sixty two. Joe's father, had been a jockey, at the now defunct Jefferson Park. His mother, Margaret Dubois, better known as Maggie, had married the handsome jockey Charlie Leblanc, in nineteen fifty nine. Three years later Joseph was born. Maggie's father, was at the time the leading trainer at Jefferson Park. Ole Speck Dubois, had been very respected in the Louisiana horse world. He primarily used the services of Joe's dad, on his racehorses. But as it sometimes happens by nineteen sixty five, Charlie, had hung up his jock boots and saddle. It was just too hard for the five foot nine inch frame to maintain the required weight. His father in law Speck, had put together a stable of cheaper horses for the retired jockey to train on the smaller tracks of southern Louisiana's bayou country. So, it was that the small family moved to the town of Carrencro, home of Cajun Downs. Carrencro, itself lay just south of Oppalousas, the town where Charlie had grown up. The area is mostly populated by descendants of the French, that settled the area along the Atchafalia Basin. Broken French, still to this day, is the language of choice, and the people, very close knit.

This is where Joe, had called home from the time he was three years old until shortly after winning that first race, when he had taken the big jump, to the New York tracks. The only time, he had ever went back, was to marry the girl, that had stolen his heart, when he had still been just a little half pint, running around the stable area of Cajun Downs.

Joe, wasn't in the big time anymore. As a matter of fact, he was at the bottom of the heap, riding broken down nags at a track in Rapid City, South Dakota. How in the world had he wound up at this hole. It still gave him a headache when he thought about it, which took him to the situation with his father. He had not spoken with his dad in a long time. These thoughts were once again haunting his soul as he was brought back to the present by the gentle hands that stroked his back. The voice of his wife softly said, "Morning, babee, and where were you just now, my love?"

"I was thinking about my father, he'll be seventy two, day after tomorrow," he said as he took his wife's hand, and led her back into their bedroom. As they walked past their full length mirror, Joe stopped, to take in the reflections of himself and Lisa Marie. He looked way past his thirty nine years. His eyes seemed hollow and distant, they held not the gleam and sparkle that they once had. His cheeks, were drawn from constant dieting. The fast life had most certainly taken it's toll. Lisa Marie, on the other hand, had held her age well, even after two children, she still maintained a petite firm body. At thirty seven, her five foot two, one hundred and ten pound frame, was just as sexy, with her dark eyes, jet black hair, flowing down her back, as the day that they had married.

"Joseph," she said, bringing him back, "you should call him, I can't imagine him not forgiving, or at least letting the past go, it has consumed both of you," she said as she brought him into her arms.

His father's words, still bit down deep in his heart. "Joseph, why, why, did you do this thing to your mother and me. I am so disgusted with you, you never let this horse run! How much did they pay you? Was it enough, Judas?"

Having said that, his father, had spit, on the ground at Joe's feet. He then turned and walked out of his son's life, leaving Joe standing there in the colors of his dad's stable, covered in mud, holding his saddle and looking so defeated in front of the grandstand of the New Orleans track. He had then handed his tack to the valet who was trying to be anywhere but there. Joe had then headed back to the jockey's quarters to shower and then head for the airport to catch his flight back to New York. That had been twelve years ago. He had not spoken with his parents since. Maggie had been very hurt with her son. She came from where family was family. You didn't turn the dollar at the cost of family and it didn't matter why.

"Thank God, your grandfather, wasn't alive to see this," she had told him when he came from the jock's room after showering. The hurt in her eyes had made him want to tell her why, but he couldn't. The game he was in had been deadly and the stakes extremely high. He wished to God that his grandfather had been alive. Speck Dubois, could have handled it. But his Papa, as he had called him, had died, the year before.

The one horse that could have taken Charlie Leblanc to the roses of the big derby in Louisville, Kentucky, had gotten beat on purpose by his own son. The horse did go, but Charlie didn't. The owners had been so furious that they had given the Derby contender to another trainer, along with the other ten horses that Charlie trained. It had been a disaster to his stable.

The secret that Joe had carried all these years, not even telling his wife why he had done the unspeakable, was eating him alive. He sometimes didn't know how he kept his sanity. His wife and children had been his rock. They were what kept him from losing it completely. He could still remember, the first time, he had seen Lisa Marie, his wife, of 20 years. It had been nineteen seventy two, just before Christmas, at Vinton Downs. A small track, that lay, just inside the Louisiana state line, twenty miles east of Beaumont, Texas.

Joe's father, had a two year old colt, that held promise as a decent runner, he wasn't going to be a world beater but he would work nicely for southern Louisiana. And Lisa Marie's father, had been a successful jockey, that plied his trade, during the winter months, at the New Orleans track, then migrated north to Chicago to ride at the more lucrative tracks during the summer. As it happened Charlie, was looking over the entry sheet for Saturday night's racing card, at Vinton Downs. He had entered the two year old colt, in a maiden race and was now scrutinizing the competition.

Charlie's horse had run second, two weeks before, and he thought that he had improved, quite a bit from his first race. The colt, was starting to get his mind on racing, instead of playing around and acting like young colts do. He was learning, what the game was really about, and he liked it.

Charlie, had named Tommy Romero, as the jockey, to ride the colt. He had ridden him in his only race, and the two had gotten along great. The colt had been a dark bay with a splash of white on his forehead, he was just under sixteen hands tall, his name was Tipsdancer, and he looked like the best bet going into the race. But nothing is a sure thing, in horse racing, that's why they call it gambling.

In the early afternoon, the Saturday before Christmas, Joe and his parents, had loaded the colt in their two horse trailer, and headed out of the stable area for the two hour journey to the Vinton track.

Joe was sitting between his parents, just about to doze off, while listening to a Hank Williams song coming out of the single speaker on the dashboard of the new Chevy pickup, his parents had bought the month before. His mother was looking over the past performances in the Daily Racing Form, which also listed the jockey's, that would ride each horse.

"Charlie; did you see who rides the Stake race tonight?" Maggie asked her husband.

"I didn't pay it much attention, Maggie," he answered while turning the radio down.

"Well, I'll tell ya, it's Gerard Fontenot; can you believe it?"

"So the big fish, comes to the little pond, what's he ridin', Maggie?"

"My lord, Charlie, when's the last time we saw him and Tracy?" she asked while trying to remember herself.

"I'd say it's been about seven years or so, wouldn't you?" he replied.

"I think so, Charlie."

"Mom, who are y'all talkin' about?" Joe asked.

Oh Joe, you were just a little ole thing, there is no way you could remember them. But they had a little baby,that you sure were fond of, what was her name Charlie?" Maggie said, then answered, her own question, "Lisa Marie, that was it, she was just the cutest baby you ever saw."

"Maggie, do you remember how Joe, was always wanting to know when we were going over to see them."

"Aw, Mom, quit it!" Joe exclaimed.

"Fact is, Maggie, I'd sure like to see them again, I kinda miss the old days when me and Gerard were riding races together."

"I know, baby, maybe we can catch him after the races. And with a little luck, Tracy might have come along."

"Sounds good, Maggie, but what I'm really hoping is that this colt, runs a good race, that's what we need," Charlie exclaimed, as he pulled the truck and trailer through the stable gate entrance of Vinton Downs, pulling to a stop, he let the window down.

"Hello, Charlie, what ya bring over this time?" the old security guard asked pointing to the trailer.

"The two-year-old colt I ran a couple of weeks ago, Tipsdancer."

"Are you staying over tonight or going back?"

"Depends on how he runs, Pete, but even if we stay the night, I'll be out of there early in the morning, my old friend."

"Well, good luck, Charlie."

"Thanks, Pete," Charlie told the old man as he pulled away from the stable entrance.

After getting the colt, settled in his stall, Charlie unhooked the trailer, while Joe and his mother sat in the truck, with the heater running.

As Charlie opened the drivers side of the truck the public address system throughout the grandstand and stable area barked out "Attention horseman would trainer Charles Leblanc, please contact the clerk of scales in the jockey's quarters right away."

"Maggie, that can't be good. I hope Red shows up soon."

Red, was the groom for Tipsdancer, he also pretty much took care of Charlie's other horses, also.

"He'll be along I'm sure, you know how dependable he is." As Maggie said this, Red's old Ford pick-up pulled in front of the receiving barn.

"How ya'll doin'? Looks like you got our champion settled in," Red said as he walked up to the Leblanc's truck. Red had worked for

Charlie about five years. But had been in the horse world for his whole forty two years. Red had never wanted to train on his own, didn't want the headaches. He was content to do exactly what he was doing, work hard, drink a little wine on Saturday night when he wasn't having to run a horse of course. Charlie Leblanc would put up with a lot but no drunks allowed. "Red we've got to go over to the front side, the clerk wants me for something, if you've got this, we'll head on over."

"I got this. Y'all, go ahead." With that, the groom added, "Les se bonto roulet," (Let the good times roll) as he was already walking, to the colts stall to ready him for tonight's race.

Pulling off, Maggie said, "We're lucky to have him, you know it, Charlie?"

"I don't want to find out what it would be like without him. I know that much." Charlie returned as they headed for the front side.

The parking lot, to the grandstand, showed that a good crowd, had turned out for the final night of racing, until after the Christmas break.

The jockeys' quarters is where the riders change into their riding silks, wait between races and, in general, spend over half of their lives.

"Maggie, y'all go on into the grandstand, by the snack bar, I'll be along directly."

"Okay, baby, you want some coffee? We're going to get a little hot chocolate, maybe a pretzel."

Joe's eyes, lit up at that, he loved those big warm pretzels, with mustard.

"I'll take some coffee, but don't y'all ruin your appetite, so we can get something to eat up in the club house." He then rustled his son's hair and added, "But I don't think a pretzel will hurt anything."

"Thanks, Dad," Joe said, smiling.

"I'll be right back ya'll," and with that said, he kissed his wife, and strode off toward the jocks room as the veterans of the game call it.

The Clerk of scales, handles all the business in the room, rider changes, weights, any problem that comes along concerning jockey's, during the races. There are good clerks, and there are bad ones.

The clerk, at Vinton Downs, was a good one named Vince Perrodin. He and Charlie had known each other for a long time.

Walking into the jock's room Charlie was met with, "Charlie Leblanc, you gotta problem, you need a rider in the eighth," Vince said as he stood up from his small desk to shake the hand of his friend.

"What's up with Tommy? Is he alright?" Charlie asked, worried about his rider.

"Yeah, he's fine, his wife had the baby. He got the call and was gone before the first race. Vince returned and then added. "Look the thirds about to run, Crystal Avant said, she'd like to ride your horse."

"I'll bet she does, Vince. That's a nice colt," Charlie said, shaking his head no.

"Charlie, you're kind of limited to what's available."

"What about Gerard Fontenot? He is here, isn't he?" Charlie asked.

"Yeah, but to ride the stake. I doubt very seriously he'll ride a ship in from Carrencro, Charlie, I know I wouldn't take the chance if I was him, would you?"

"Just let me talk to him and see what he has to say about it. You know he and I go back a long way. He knows I wouldn't get him hurt."

"Okay, I'll get him Charlie, wait here." Vince then went around the corner to the dressing and shower room. "Fontenot; come here a minute, would ya?"

"Hey, Vince, who's gonna ride that open horse in the eighth?" asked Crystal Avant

"I think he might be coming now Crystal," Vince said with a smile.

"Whoa, just a minute, I'm here to ride the stake, which I should win, and then I'm gone, back to New Orleans." Gerard said.

"Well the trainer, wants to ask you himself, so just humor him then say no, if you want to, he's around the corner there."

"Oh, alright, Vince, if it'll make you happy," Gerard said as he rounded the corner.

Charlie had his back turned to Gerard as the rider said, "Excuse me, but I'm not going to be able to ride—well, I'll be a drowned rat."

"Hello, Charlie, God, it's been a long time, is it your horse that needs a rider?"

"Yeah, I'm in a bind. Look, Gerard, the colt's alright. I wouldn't put you in a bad spot and I think the horse will win."

"Alright then, Vince, name me as the rider on Charlie's horse."

"Gotcha covered, jock. I gotta go check the third in."

And with that, the clerk, stepped out of the door.

"Gerard, how's the family, Tracy, your little girl?"

"Doing great, as a matter of fact, they're here tonight."

"No kiddin', Maggie and Joe are up in the grandstand. I know she'll want to see Tracy."

"Well, they're on the second floor, why don't you see if y'all can find 'em and I'll see you in the paddock for the eighth."

"Thanks Gerard, this really helps me out a lot, and really, the colt is good, I promise."

"I believe you, Charlie, now I gotta get back in the room and start getting ready."

"See ya in a bit Gerard," Charlie said as the two shook hands again. And then Charlie turned walking out the jocks room.

Charlie, found his wife and son, sharing a pretzel and sipping hot chocolate as he walked into the grandstand.

At that moment, the Announcer spoke, into the P.A. system. "We have a jockey change in the eighth race tonight, the number five horse Tipsdancer, will now be ridden by Gerard Fontenot, make the rider, Gerard Fontenot, there are no more changes on tonights card."

Walking up to Maggie and Joe, his wife handed him his black coffee in a Styrofoam cup saying, "Well sounds like you found Gerard, how come he's ridin' Tip, tonight? Tommy's alright, isn't he?" she asked.

"Just fine Maggie, his wife had their baby, so he took off. Anyway, I needed a rider and thank God, he was here."

"Did you ask him about Tracy?" Maggie asked

"Sure did, matter of fact, she's up on the second floor, let's see if we can find her."

Walking toward the stairs Maggie, saw her first. "There she is Charlie, she hasn't changed a bit."

Tracy, was descending the stairs that led from the second floor clubhouse section of the grandstand with a dark haired beauty, of about eight or so holding her hand, when she saw Maggie's waving hand.

As they came together. "I can't believe it, when I heard Gerard was named to ride another horse tonight, I knew it had to be an old friend. And there it was when I looked it up in the program. I couldn't believe it," exclaimed Tracy Fontenot.

"How have y'all been, Tracy? Lord, is this Lisa Marie? She's growing right on up," said Maggie.

Lisa, not being shy, even at the tender age of eight, stepped right up front, with her hand out, "My name's Lisa Marie Fontenot. Do I know you?" she asked, Maggie, in a matter of fact way.

"Well, hello, Lisa Marie. I'm Maggie, and this is my husband, Charlie, and my son, Joe," Maggie said warmly taking the little girl's hand.

"She's not shy by a longshot," said Tracy with a small laugh, adding, "How have y'all been Maggie?"

"We're doing good, bought a home in Carrencro, settled down," Maggie said.

Little Joe Leblanc, for the first time in his life, was speechless and his chest felt like it would burst; however, his mind was saying, this is the prettiest girl you have ever seen. That was his first impression of Lisa Marie and after almost thirty years he still felt that way.

The friends had gone up to the clubhouse to talk over old times. Lisa Marie and Joseph were getting to know each other with Lisa doing most of the talking and Joe, not being able to look her in the eye for very long at a time.

"Well, ladies, I've got to go saddle a winner, I hope," Charlie said as he stood up from the table and adding. "Joe, you coming to the paddock?"

"Yes, sir, Dad, can Lisa come?"

"It's pretty cold down there but—"

"Charlie, she can stay with us you'll have your hands full down there," Tracy said, with a knowing smile and Charlie mouthing, *Thank you.*

"That's okay, Mr. Charlie, I'll stay up here where it's warm," Lisa said, sounding all grown up.

By the time Charlie and Joe got to the paddock, Red, had already gotten the colt into the number five slot to be saddled.

"Hey, Red, how's he doin'?" asked Charlie of the 2-year-old.

"Good, boss, he's ready. I think we have us a winner. I heard Fontenot's going to ride him."

The Valets, had come out of the jock's room and were making their way toward the horses they would help saddle. After getting the colt saddled, Red, took him for a short walk to stretch around the paddock walking ring. At that moment the jockey's, came out also to talk with the trainers of their perspective mounts.

"Hello, Charlie," Gerard said as he walked up to slot five with his hand out for the customary handshake between rider and trainer.

"Gerard, thanks again, I really think we can win this."

"How do you want me to ride him?"

"I'd like you to lay off the pace, maybe three or four back then make one run, he's push button, Gerard, and he's got some kick. If it pieces together different do what you think's best."

"Sounds good."

"Rider's up," the official called. And, with that, Charlie, legged his at one time best friend into the saddle."

"Good luck, Gerard, be safe."

"Let's win one," Gerard answered as he took up the reins and settled his feet into the irons of his jock's saddle.

The horses are coming on to the track for the running of the eighth race tonight. Number one is Ocala Flash, ridden by Jose Hernandez, number two horse Sea Breeze, with Tommy Hughes, in the saddle, number three Alligator Point, with Sammy Cox to ride, the four horse is Road Rage, with jockey Patrick Murray, the five, Tipsdancer, with Gerard Fontenot, number six Marty's Graw, with jockey Randy Hebert, the seven, Itsallgood, with Stori Peyton set to ride.

After watching the post parade, Charlie and Joseph made their way back up to the second floor of the grandstand to where the ladies were.

The announcer, calmly said, "The horses are moving, into the starting gate for the eighth race, a six furlong dash."

"Here we go," said, Charlie, as they all looked out through the glass that covered the whole second floor view to the track.

"They're all in line, the flag is up, and they're off!!!" the announcer said, excitedly.

"Racing down the backside Sea Breeze with Tommy Hughes, has clearly gotten loose on the front end by a length and a half, with Itsallgood, in second, that's Ocala Flash, coming up on the outside, followed by Tipsdancer…stay close, don't let the speed get away Gerard," Charlie said, softly to himself as he watched his horse in fourth place with lots of race to run.

"They blazed the first quarter in twenty two and change as Sea Breeze, still with the lead, heads into the far turn, Itsallgood, still right there in second, moving up into third is Tipsdancer, and Gerard Fontenot…"

Gerard himself was thinking, the pace is way to fast, it's got to back up, so he would wait to make his move he decided.

"Ladies, it looks like we're in good position, he's in third with dead aim on the leaders," Charlie said.

"Just inside the three-eighths pole Itsallgood, moves up to challenge Seabreeze, who is starting to fade, that's Tipsdancer, right there tucked in on the rail." The announcer was beginning to get excited at the makings of a good horse race with a dramatic finish.

Gerard, had eased Tipsdancer, into second place and was still hugging the rail, Sea Breeze, had faded back to fifth place as Alligator Point, moved into third and was beginning his stretch run.

"C'mon big colt it's time to go, son," Gerard told his mount as he turned Tipsdancer loose.

Stori Peyton, had gone to the whip trying to fend off Tipsdancer's bid for the lead. Marty's Graw, had swung wide coming out of the turn and was trying to run down the leaders. Alligator Point was making a strong run in third place.

"C'mon, c'mon—get up there, Tip!" Maggie was urging excitedly as she stood up from the table.

"That's it, Gerard, get into him!" said Charlie as he also got up from the table.

"Yeah! My daddy's going to win again!" Lisa Marie said, jumping up and down, Joe also was getting into the supercharged finish. Tracy, was the only one who wasn't on her feet cheering her husband on toward the finish line.

"With less than a sixteenth of a mile to go, Itsallgood and Tipsdancer, head and head, stride for stride as they race for the wire."

Gerard had known the colt had another gear, and years of riding races had told him it was now that he should ask for it, so reaching back he tapped the colt with his whip, the colt responded with penned ears as he dug in.

"Inside the seventy yard pole it's Tipsdancer, pulling away from Itsallgood, with Alligator Point, right there but it's all…Tipsdancer at the wire!!!"

"He did it, y'all, I knew he could win, let's go down for the picture," Charlie said, proudly.

Joseph, could still remember how happy they had been that night.

"Joe, you better snap out of it," Lisa Marie said, to her husband, then added, "You're going to be late to the jock's room, what's your first race today?" she asked, as she kissed Joe's cheek, sliding her hands around his waist and looking into his eyes.

"I ride the last four, so Mrs. Leblanc, is there something you might like to do for an hour or so?"

"The kids have left for school," she returned, stepping into his body even more so, to where she could feel his hardness, then pulling away to lead him to their bed.

Joseph, had always made her feel unbelievable in bed, and this time, would be no different. These two truly loved each other. It was apparent in everything they did.

"Joe, I love you so much," his wife said as she lay in his arms after making love.

He kissed, her forehead, as he told her, "You are everything to me Lisa, forever and ever."

Thinking of his love for her took him back to that night at Vinton Downs.

They had all went down to the winners circle to get in the win picture, it was a very happy moment, the race itself was just a cheap maiden race, but the camaraderie of old friends, is what held it special.

Dismounting Tipsdancer, Gerard had hugged his friend Charlie, saying, "It was a nice ride, thanks Charlie."

"No, thank you, Gerard."

"Where will y'all be after the stake?" asked Gerard

"Why don't we meet you outside the jock's room right after the last race," Charlie said as Red led the gelding off to the test barn for the mandatory urine test.

"Sounds good," the jockey, said adding, "I've got to get to the room to get ready for the next race, see y'all in a bit." He then kissed his wife on the cheek and hugged his little girl Lisa, and then turned and made his way back to the jock's room.

"Maggie, I'm going to help Red with Tip, y'all go back in where it's warm, I'll be back in a little bit," Charlie told his wife.

After Charlie had walked off, the ladies along with Lisa and Joseph had gone back up to the clubhouse to watch Gerard ride the feature.

"Tracy, you looked worried during the stretch run of our race, what's going on? Are you alright? I mean you use to get excited when we were all in New Orleans and Gerard would make the lead." Maggie asked while the kids went to order some hot chocolate.

"I'll tell you, Maggie, you know the deal, it's not a matter of if a jockey will get hurt, but when, and how badly, and lately, I feel like the odds are stacked against Gerard. He's gone for awhile now without a spill and that scares me. My gut feeling isn't good, that's why Lisa and myself came over tonight. I can hardly watch, but I can't be far from him either."

"How long have you felt this way?"

"Just about two weeks is all, there was this apprentice,, in Kentucky that went down in a spill about three weeks ago and was paralyzed from the waist down, I keep thinking that's going to happen to Gerard."

"Have you told Gerard how you feel?"

"No, I have not and I more than likely want. It's just something I'll have to get over, it comes with the territory of being a jock's wife, you know how it is Maggie."

"Look, Lisa, the horses are coming on to the track," Joe said as the two walked back up to the table where their mothers were."

"There's my dad, he's the number two this time, isn't he, Mom?"

"Yes, sweetheart, he is."

The horse that Gerard was riding, had won his last two races in New Orleans, even though they had been small overnight handicaps, he looked like much the best for the stake race that night. The patrons had sure backed him at the mutuals, betting him down to three to one.

As they moved into the starting gate, Charlie, made his way back to the clubhouse. "Well, Tip came back in good shape, acted like he just went for a walk in the park," he told the ladies, then asked, "What numbers Gerard, Maggie?"

"The two horse," she answered.

"They're all in line—they're off and running!" The announcer called.

From the very moment that Joe, had received the phone call on how to ride his dad's horse in New Orleans, the day he had gotten the big horse beat, he had played and replayed what had transpired in the stake race that his father in law Gerard, had won. As a matter of fact, it was yet something else that haunted him for many years.

After the races that night both family's had driven into Beaumont to have a midnight supper, but first they had decided to stay the night.

So they had checked into room's that were side by side at the Holiday Inn, on Interstate 10, on the east side of Beaumont, Texas. They had then went to the Red Barn twenty four hour restaurant, that was a favorite of the people from the track.

Joe, that night had fallen asleep, with his head on his mother's lap, as they followed the Fontenots back to the motel. He didn't remember actually getting into bed, for his dad must have carried him into the room while he was asleep. However, he did remember waking up to the sounds of his dad talking with someone on the telephone in the room. And then he sat up, to see Lisa Marie, at the foot of his bed, her head on a pillow and sleeping soundly with the covers pulled up to her chin.

Her mother was sitting in one of the chairs while Maggie, was saying something that he didn't understand completely, it had something to do with Lisa's dad.

"Mom, what's going on? Is everything alright?"

"Yes, Joe, everything's fine, now you go back to sleep, darling."

"Maggie, Tracy, the police, will be here in a minute, I'm going outside to meet them."

Joe couldn't go back to sleep, he knew something bad had happened he just didn't know what. However in the next couple of hours he had pieced some things together. For one, Lisa's dad, had gone back out to the foodmart for something, he didn't know for what, only that he hadn't come back and it was now eight a.m.

Lisa's mother was worried sick and crying. Maggie was trying to calm her down, but she just kept saying, "I knew something wasn't right, something bad has happened to Gerard."

And indeed something had happened. The police had came back at about 10:00 a.m. Joe's father had gone to the track and had not yet returned from taking care of Tipsdancer.

Lisa Marie was coming out of the bathroom when the policeman was saying to her mother, "Ma'am, we need you to identify your husband, Mrs. Fontenot." Tracy had begun screaming, and from that moment, time stood still or at least to Joe, it seemed as though it had. Even though he himself was just barely ten years old, he held and comforted Lisa Marie, as much as he could. In the years to come they had comforted each other with an unconditional love.

Over the next couple of days, these things came to light. Gerard for one had been found down an old dirt lane slumped over the steering wheel of the Fontenots' Buick, he had been shot twice in the back of the head, an apparent robbery victim. No arrest had been made and the police had no clues to who could have done it. The last person it was believed to have seen Gerard was the clerk at the all night food mart where Gerard had bought a pack of Marlboros and a Dr. Pepper, that had been at about one a.m. He had left the motel room at about twelve forty five, leaving only about fifteen minutes for error. That wasn't much to go on.

The funeral had been held in Belle Chase, Louisiana where Gerard had been raised. As for Tracy, she was lost, she didn't know where she was going to go or what she was going to do. She had always depended on Gerard to take care of her and Lisa Marie. They had saved some money through the years but it wasn't enough to last a life time. She needed a plan. Tracy couldn't go back to New Orleans, there were to many memories for her and Lisa. What they needed was a fresh place to start and to mend. And well, the Leblancs, being the kind of people they were, very adamant, insisting that Tracy and Lisa stay with them until a game plan had been put together or for as long as they needed. Even though the two families had not seen each other in some years, that didn't matter. The Leblancs considered Tracy and Lisa family.

It wasn't long, however, that a game plan had been devised at the hands of Speck Dubois, and his daughter Maggie.

What Cajun Downs needed was a tack and horseman's supply store that would be convenient for the trainers stabled on the grounds. So, with money from the Fontenots' savings, some from the Leblancs' meager account, and a little help from Speck, an older mobile home was purchased, gutted, then shelves added and a deal struck with Cajun Downs Stable area at the urging of Maggie's father's friends, with let's say, a little clout. The winner's circle tack supply had opened with Tracy and Maggie at the helm.

Tracy, had soon bought a small home in Carrencro that she and Lisa Marie had moved into, to start their new life.

From those days on, Joseph and Lisa Marie were inseparable, they had become best friends, still were. He could even remember their first real kiss. It had been the night of his first win as a jockey. She had told him,"I guess you'll be going off to New York to ride, like you've always wanted Joe, there want be any room for a fourteen year old kid, in your life, your going places, and I will always love you," she had said, these things, with tears in her eyes.

"Lisa, you will always be, the most important thing in my life, no matter how far I go. I'm coming back to get you, you'll see," and then he nervously moved his lips toward hers, she moved into his arms and they kissed passionately for the first time. Joe, at that moment, had found something far greater than winning races, he had found the tender kisses, of Lisa Marie Fontenot, his future wife.

"Joe, I could lay here with you all day, for the rest of my life, however we wouldn't get much done," Lisa was saying, as she snuggled into her husband.

"Oh, yes, we would. That's a fact." He returned grinning, then added, "But I better go ride a few races or we might have to really live off of love." With that said, he kissed Lisa Marie, then got up to head for the shower.

"You better hurry, Joe, it's almost one o'clock. You want me to drive you?" she asked

"Yeah, if you don't mind picking me up, also, after school's out, maybe you and the kids could catch the last race I ride."

"That sounds good, honey pie." But she doubted that he heard her for the shower was already running.

Returning from the shower, Joe was slipping on a pair of jeans, with Lisa in the kitchen, putting together some fruit for Joe to take to the jock's room to munch on while he waited for the perspective races that he would ride. Joe had to watch his weight pretty close. Although he had a different method, which he was now lining out on a small mirror he kept in a drawer by the bed just for this purpose, rolling up a dollar bill, he snorted one of the two lines of puruvian

Plake, just as the phone rang. "Can you get that honey?" His wife called out.

"I got it." He returned, placing the bill on the night stand and grabbing the remote with one hand to turn down the television, with the other, he reached for the telephone receiver.

"Hello," he said. "Hey there, Joe, long time no see. You know what they say, you can run, but you can't hide!" said the voice, followed by laughter.

"What do you want!" Joe asked in an agitated voice.

"Why Joe, is that anyway to talk, to an old friend?"

"You're no friend, matter of fact, you're the enemy!"

"Now, you listen to me, you Cajun reject, today in the seventh race, you don't finish no where close to the front, understand? Oh, one more thing, jock, your mom's still gettin' around good. Let's make sure it stay's that way."

"Don't you go near her. Do you hear me?"

"You just ride 'em like your told, you hear that?" Click, the receiver went dead.

"Who was that, Joe?" Lisa Marie asked from the kitchen.

"Somebody wantin' to know if I could breeze a horse for them tomorrow morning." He couldn't tell her the truth, but he hated lying.

"You ready, Joe. It's time to go."

On the way to the track, passing the Roger's Dude Ranch and nightly rodeo, Joe looked out to the ex-presidents faces of Mount Rushmore, and wondering how long it would be before they had to move again. Their average time at a new track was about two seasons. You just couldn't keep getting favorites beat, pretty soon you wouldn't be riding anything at all.

All to together they had moved a total of eight times in twelve years. He wondered where they would go next. Lisa Marie herself had wondered why they kept moving but finally she had attributed it to the fact that Joe, just got tired of riding at the same place, it was like he was running from something, and in fact he was—himself among others.

The moves themselves were getting hard on their children, which were at the age where they needed a lot of stability as they went through highschool.

Their oldest was fifteen, Lanette Lene't Leblanc, had been born in Yew York, while Joe, had been on his way to being the leading jockey in the nation in both wins and money eared for the third time in his career. Life had been so sweet back then. Lanette, was a beauty, taking after her mother, with dark hair, her eyes though were green, unlike her moms, her facial features as well as her body were shaping up to be a replica of Lisa Marie. She was smart and very popular whenever they moved to a new town, it didn't take her anytime at all to meet new friends. Still, Joe knew, that it was hard on her, even though she never complained. She was a true little trooper. It was a shame that she had been deprived her grandparents while she was growing up.

Lisa and Joe's son, Bradly Jon Leblanc, had just turned eleven and was the spittin' image of his dad.

He to was a good kid that never gave his parents any trouble. He had stated when he was about eight that he wanted to be a jockey, like his father. That was something that scared the livin' daylights out of Joe.

Pulling into the racetrack Lisa Marie said, "Honey; do you know somebody in a blue Suburban?"

"I don't know, why?" he answered.

"Well, there's one behind, us flashing his lights. I think they want us to stop."

Panic gripped Joe, all he could think about was the phone call he had received earlier. "Don't stop, Lisa, step on it!!!

"What the hell are you talkin' about, Joe? Who is that?" As she to was reacting to Joe's apparent panic, Lisa also started to panic, although she hadn't known why, or why Joe, seemed so scared, but it was scaring her also.

At that moment, another suburban, darted in front of the Leblanc's Bronco causing Lisa Marie, to slam on the brakes. What happened next was something similar to a Miami Vice drug bust.

Guys, big guys, were rushing toward the Bronco, with guns drawn, and yelling, "Out of the car now, keep your hands where we can see 'em, now,now, move, move it! And then Lisa and Joe, were dragged, from their vehicle.

More shouting from the men, that to Lisa Marie, it sounded like they said, they were the FBI. The only thing that was going through her mind as her Cajun anger built was, "What in the hell, have you done this time, Joseph Leblanc?

Joe, however, was just as confused, at what was going on as his wife was. Surely this couldn't be over a couple of grams of coke and that's when it hit him. The phone call, the FBI, all the years of defrauding the public, by not letting some horses win, even if he had done those things out of fear.

"What in the hell, is all this about? Who the hell, are you people?" Lisa Marie screamed, at the agents as they herded them into the suburban parked in front of their Bronco.

"Ma'am, settle down, we'll explain once we're out of the area," returned one of the agents who seemed to be in charge.

"At least tell us who you are. This is crazy," a bewildered Joe said.

"Mr. Leblanc, we're with the Federal Bureau of Investigation and you, my friend, are in a lot of trouble.

"Joe, what have you done?" asked Lisa Marie, with tears in her eyes. They had been handcuffed, stuffed in the back seat of the suburban. One of the agents had jumped in the Leblanc's vehicle and was now following them. Where they were, Joe nor Lisa Marie knew, until they pulled into the Best Western motel. "What are we doing here?" Joe asked, as they stopped in front of room 151.

Once in the room, one of the agents, began to speak. "Okay, Mr.and Mrs. Leblanc, we're going to remove the cuffs, but don't try anything stupid, alright?" Lisa and Joe nodded their heads simultaneously–yes.

"Good, now my name is Agent Russo, and before we go any farther, Joseph G. Leblanc, you are under arrest for race fixing, fraud, and conspiracy to commit fraud, you have the right to remain silent, but

I promise you, it want be in your best interest, you have the right to a lawyer, if you can't afford one, one will be appointed to you, do you understand what I have just said?"

"Yes, but—" Joe started, but was interrupted by Russo.

"Before you say anything, we have tapes from phone conversations, tapes of races, we've got you dead to rights, the only thing that we don't have is, who you're working with or for."

"Joseph Leblanc, you had better tell me that this is one big mistake," shot Lisa Marie as she sat on the side of one of the two beds that were in the room.

"Lisa, it's a very long story."

"Well, you best get started telling it then, don't you think?" she asked, and then before he could answer, she directed another question toward Russo, "am I under arrest for anything detective or whatever you are?"

"No ma'am, however some things are going to have to be worked out before anyone leaves this room."

"Look, Mr. Russo, we gotta talk," Joe said.

"Yes, we do Mr Leblanc, we've had you under surveillance about three years now, we have wire tapes from conversations with someone we have dubbed as the Headless Horseman, we gave him that name because we have no idea who he is, all we have is a voice. The one other thing that we're not sure of is, you don't even know who it is yourself. However, before it's over, we will get to the bottom of this."

Joe's mind went back to the death of Lisa's father Gerard, when Joe had gotten that first phone call the morning he was flying out of New York to New Orleans to ride the best colt his dad had ever trained, in the southern Derby. It had been April of nineteen eighty six, and every night for the past week, Charlie Leblanc, had called his son, from New Orleans, to make sure that Joe, was coming to ride the big red colt and to tell him how good the horse was. Charlie had been so excited and so was his mother Maggie. Joe also was excited for his parents. He himself had been riding some of the best horses in the country, he had won the Derby that runs on the first Saturday of May the year before. That was his dream come true and now from the way his dad talked he might just win it again for his parents this time.

That Saturday morning, all had seemed normal for that time of year. Meaning that Joe was constantly flying out to ride a stakes race somewhere, sometimes it seemed as though he lived on an airplane.

He had just stepped out of the shower when the phone rang in their Long Island home, "Hello," Joe spoke into the telephone.

"You will not speak, you will only listen, and when I'm finished I'm hanging up. Then the decision is yours. Now, Joseph, I want you to remember back to the night that Gerard Fontenot was killed, all these years everyone has thought that it had been a robbery, not so, he was told to do certain things that he didn't comply with, he paid a dear price for his actions and now with that said, I will tell you as he had been told, today you will not win a certain race in Louisiana, if you do, well then, let the blood of ones you hold very dear to your heart be on your hands…" The voice had stopped and the phone went dead, leaving Joe staring at the handset like it was a serpent.

He had heard about phone calls such as these but he himself had never received one until then.

"Mr. Leblanc, your to ride a horse today in the seventh and we already know that you received a call about forty five minutes ago telling you not to finish anywhere near the front end, the Headless Horseman, then made reference to your mother, and has always made a similar comment in all of his calls. Look Leblanc, do you know this guy? If you do, then do you want to work with us on this?

It could cut your time way down to where it might bottom out."

"Mr. Russo, the guy that called me, I have no idea who it is, I only know that his threat is against my mother."

"Can I call you Joe?" asked Russo.

"Sure, I don't care."

"Alright, we can provide protection for your mon, the rest of your family, should be safe."

"I'd think so, I'd have to say that whoever it is, they are in Louisiana, we're a long way from Carrencro, where my mom is."

"Okay, Joe, can you win the seventh race? If you do we can more than likely get the Headless Horseman to make a move."

"And what, Russo, use my mom as bait? You can't be serious."

"Mr. Leblanc, I'd say, the only other choice you have is—let's play go to jail."

"Joseph, I think you should do as they say. I know now why everything has gone to hell, you've carried this around no telling how long. Let's end it," Lisa Marie said with pleading eyes as she touched her husband's hand.

"Lisa, this thing goes a lot farther than just what we've said right here, and you're right baby, actually I'm glad that this is about to be over."

What Joe or Lisa or the FBI didn't know was, it was a long way from being over.

"Okay, we need to move! What I want y'all to do is take your vehicle and go to the track, Mrs. Leblanc, were you planning on staying at the track today or did you have other plans?"

"I was going to pick up our children and then come back to watch the last few races," Lisa answered.

"Okay, we'll do just what you had planned."

"Good. Now, Joe, where will your mom be abut now?" asked the FBI agent.

"Russo, I have no idea, I would imagine she'd be home, though you have to understand, I have not talked with my parents in a very long time."

"Joe, I've talked to her, from time to time, she'll be home in Carrencro, the address is—seventeen thirty four Sunset Rd. Don't look so shocked Joseph, surely you wouldn't think that she and I wouldn't at least talk, once in a while?"

The agent had then ushered the Leblancs out of the room and into their vehicle, saying, "Joe, we will be watching you and also we have a lot more talking to do."

And with that Lisa and Joe had pulled out of the motel parking lot heading back to the track. Talk, was very little, as they were both lost deep into their thoughts.

Joe had gotten out of the bronco in front of the racing office which connected to the jocks' room.

"Lisa, I am so sorry about all of this."

"Wait, Joe, only tell me one thing, that's all I want, did you do this for money or drugs or whatever or were you threatened into it?"

"Lisa, you just don't know the half of it, but I never did this voluntarily. I gotta go, know in your heart that I love you very much."

"I love you, too, Joe. I'll be back in a little while with the kids. You be careful out there today, you hear me?" She then leaned over to kiss her husband.

Joe entered the jocks' room. with little fan fare, other than the clerk of scales yelling. "Well it's about time, Leblanc, I was going to give you another ten minutes then you were being taken off of your mounts."

"Sorry I'm late. Something came up, but my weight's okay," Joe said as he rushed to get into his riding gear.

Thirty minutes later, Joe stood in the paddock, talking with the trainer of the horse he was to ride in the seventh.

"Hello, Joe, how ya doin' today?" the trainer asked.

"I'm good, Will. Yourself?" returned Joe.

"Couldn't be better, looks like we should win this pretty easy."

"A walk in the park," Joe told Will, as the official, barked, "Riders up!"

Joe, himself, was thinking, as he took up the reins, God, I hope everything turns out alright. He had even contemplated throwing the race but then he trusted that the FBI, had the situation, well in hand.

As they loaded in the gate, Joe, took a deep breath and let it out and the old Joe Leblanc, said, to himself, let's go win one, big boy! And, in fact, when he turned for home, he was in second place, a split second later he was in front and driving for the wire, when he crossed the wire, he was the winner. After the races, he came out of the jocks' room, looking for Lisa and the kids. He didn't spot them, however, he did see the bronco, just abut the time that, by now, a well known blue suburban pulled up in front of him. It was Agent Russo.

"Hey, Joe, we've got people all over your mother, nobody can hurt her, believe me, she's safe."

"That's great, have you seen my wife?"

"No, I just got here," the agent returned.

"There's our bronco, looks like something is on the windshield," Joe said, walking up to the bronco, he saw that it indeed was a note, picking it off of the wiper blade, his first look, brought his heart to a stop, for this is what he read. "Joseph, Joseph, your decision did cost you dearly, you see, I only commented about your mother, ah, but the game's not over, just the stakes higher, I'll be in touch." Joe could not believe what he was reading, his breath was short, his chest hurt, and all he could do was hand the agent the note.

Russo read it very careful and then reached for his cell phone, that was clipped to his waist belt. He spoke several sharp words that Joe didn't comprehend but then he wasn't understanding anything, other than, he had made a grave mistake, in winning the seventh race, now his wife and children were in danger, if not, dead.

Russo stayed on the phone for about two minutes then ended the call.

"Mr. Leblanc, I'm sorry, we thought the Headless Horseman, was in Louisiana…"

"Sorry, sorry, is that all you can say, you're sorry! Let me tell you about sorry." And without any warning, Joe, even as he said, those words, was aiming a blow, to the agents nose which connected, knocking the agent Russo backward, the two agents that had been with Russo, quickly gathered Joe up and held him at bay.

"Russo, if anything happens to my family—" Joe was saying when he heard someone cry out his name from behind him. They all turned in the direction of the woman's voice.

"Joe—Joseph! What's going on?" It was Lisa Marie with Lannett and Bradly right beside her.

"Lisa, kids, oh thank god, you're alright, where have y'all been?" Joe asked, as he shook free, of the agents grasp.

"We were in the grandstand, watching the last race, when this guy, comes up to me and says that we're supposed to meet you, thirty minutes after the last race, at the far end of the grandstand, and not to leave until you come to get us."

"Mrs. Leblanc, what did this man look like?" asked Agent Russo.

"Like one of you, he had a dark suit on, dark glasses, I thought he was one of y'all, that's why, I never questioned it. Joe, what's wrong, you look like you've seen a ghost." Lisa Marie said.

"Damn!" said Russo, as he started punching number's into his cell phone. "Hello, yeah, this is Russo. I need you to stay on Mrs. Leblanc...you did what, get back over there now!" Russo said, "Do you hear me?" With that, he disconnected.

"What's going on, Mom!" asked Lannett, with a worried look on her face. "It's okay, honey, I'll explain later." Lisa Marie told her daughter.

"Mr. Leblanc, I hate having to do this, however I have no choice. You have broken the law, so I have to take you into custody," Agent Russo was saying, as his cell phone rang.

"Hello," he said and then listened with an attentive look that soon turned to a frown. "Joseph, what do you want me to do?" asked his wife.

"I'm not sure, I guess they'll set bail, so don't let me sit in there, as a matter of fact, I need you to call Harry Wellman, in New York, tell him what's happened and see if he can refer you to an attorney, here in Rapid City. His number is in the Rolodex at home," Joseph told his wife, these things, as Agent Russo ended his call.

"Mr. Leblanc," said Russo. "I have some bad news. Your mom's missing. We can't locate her."

"What do you mean, you can't locate her?" Blurted Joe.

"Somehow, it looks like there are two members of the Headless Horseman when they ran a decoy here to pull us off your mother by making us think they had your wife and kids."

"Russo, you told me this wouldn't happen."

"I'm sorry, but look, we're still going to take you into custody. It's the law; however, we have agent's all over Lafayette and Carrencro, looking for your mother..."

"Like hell!" Joe said, and then something happened to his brain. He didn't know why because one minute after he had bolted away from the group, he wished he hadn't, but it was too late. So he kept running, through the parking lot, between cars, when he spotted a man getting into a Pontiac Trans Am, he rushed the man, knocking him out of the way, as he did, he grabbed the keys from the bewildered guy, and in a flash, was in the drivers seat with the door shut and locked, just as the three agents reached the car but they were to late and to far away from their suburban. Joe fired up the Trans Am and gunned it out of the parking lot, he rounded the curve that led back to where his bronco was parked, he pulled up to Lisa Marie, just long enough to say, "I'll be in touch. Call Harry. I'll leave a message. I love y'all!" And then, he was gone, leaving Lisa Marie and the children standing by the bronco. Lisa was scared, but she knew that her husband, was doing what he thought best. She silently prayed for Joe, as tears ran down her cheeks. As the agents ran back up to her, one of them started to jump in the suburban but was stopped short when Russo said ! Sam forget it, he'll surface, he want leave his family behind for very long."

"That's where you underestimate my husband, Mr. Russo. He's on a mission and God help the person who has done something to his mother," Lisa Marie said in defense of her husband.

"What did he say to you? He told you something?" questioned Russo.

"Yeah, he did. He said he loved us. Now, Agent Russo, if I'm not under arrest, my children and I are going home now." And without waiting for Russo's answer, she pushed past him and unlocked the door to the Bronco.

Meanwhile, on the second floor of the grandstand, a figure stood watching the scene that had just transpired and thought, "Well, well, the rabbit jumped the gun," and then, replacing his dark glasses, he punched a number into his cell phone. On the other end, a voice asked, "Has it begun?"

"Yes ma'am, the rabbit's on the run."

"What about the rabbit's family?"

"They just drove off."

"Good, very good, now I need you back in Louisiana right away."

"Yes, ma'am, I'm on my way." Then the voice had ended the call while thinking, *Finally, this thing is coming to an end.*

Only she didn't know that it wasn't going to be very quick or easy.

Joe was on the interstate heading toward North Dakota, and as he rolled through Sturgis, he was thinking. "What in the hell am I doing? This is crazy!" But his mind was already working. If he could just get to Buffalo, South Dakota, forty miles up the road. What he needed now, was to change cars, right then, his mind changed gears and he changed lanes to make the last exit for Sturgis.

Joe had been buying coke, off of this biker in Sturgis, for about a year now. The guy, always had an old truck or car of some sort around his house, that he had taken as collateral in a dope deal, and more times than not, the people, that owned the automobiles, never got them back. As he pulled into the drive way, he could see, that he was in luck.

"Hey Goose," Joe said, to the man stepping off the porch as Joe himself exited the Trans Am.

"Goose, I need a big favor man, I need to borrow a car to go to Buffalo!"

"Hell, what's wrong with the one you're drivin?"

"Don't shoot me, Goose, but it's hot. Look, man, some things have happened and I need to get to Louisiana. My mom's in some real danger."

"Hey, say no more, only tell me why, Buffalo? That's in the opposite way of Louisiana."

"Yeah, but there's a cowboy who flies to a lot of rodeo's who lives there. I'm hopin' he's home. He owes me a couple of favors on tips I gave him at the races."

"Joe, here, you know his number, call 'em, if he's there, we'll get you there."

"Thanks, Goose, I'll never forget this," Joe said as he took the cell phone, then from his wallet, he produced a business card that read Chris Johnson Rodeo Cowboy at large with a phone number, which Joe, quickly punched into the phone.

"Hello," a voice said on the other end.

"Hello, Chris?"

"That's me, who's this?"

"Joe Leblanc, Chris."

Meanwhile, Lisa Marie and the children, were back at home. Lannett, was in the living room trying not to cry, Bradly, was glued to his mother, not letting her out of his sight. The boy was scared, he had never seen anything like what he had witnessed earlier, but then they were all scared.

Lisa had retrieved the Lawyer's telephone number and was now dialing it when she remembered the wire tap that the F.B.I. had on their phone. "Damn," she said

"C'mon kids, we're going over to Suzy's." Suzy was an older lady, that Lisa had made friends with, about the second week, that they had lived in Rapid City. Suzy had came by one afternoon to welcome them to the neighbor hood. The two had gotten along well ever since.

Joe had made two call's from Goose's place, one to the cowboy Chris Johnson, the other to Harry Wellman, he had told Harry, that Lisa would be calling, and to give her this message, it's a rainy day, twenty one fifty seven, he had told Harry, that she would know what to do, and that she could explain more about what was going on, he himself, was on the run and had to go. He had then ended the call, not giving Harry, a chance to ask any questions. Harry had been a friend to Joseph Leblanc, since the first week that the then sixteen year old Joe, had walked with his agent, into the barn of Dewy Stevens, at the New York track. Harry had nine horses under Dewy's care. Joe had won his first race in the Big Apple on one of those nine horses and eventually rode everything that Dewy sent to the post, the combination of owner, trainer, and jockey had produced records, that may never be broken.

Joe pulled into the airstrip of Buffalo, South Dakota to find Chris Johnson standing beside his four seater cessna.

Goose had driven Joe up to Buffalo himself in an old ford pick-up after promising to deliver the Trans Am to the truck stop up on the interstate and then to call the police telling them where it was at, so that the owner could retrieve it.

"Goose, thanks a lot, you really came thru for me, I owe you one." Joe told the biker as he stepped from the pickup.

"Naw, man, you owe me, too, but who's countin', right? Adios, mi amigo." And then Goose pulled off.

"Hello, Chris, I can't thank you enough for this."

"Hell, it's alright, I'm supposed to be in San Antonio, day after tomorrow, might as well head south a little early." And with having said that, the two boarded the small plane and taxied off down the narrow strip.

"Well, hello, there Lisa, children, c'mon in, how are ya'll doin'?" asked Suzy as she opened the door for her visitors.

Suzy was about fifty one, had fire red hair and green eyes, just as grandmotherly a woman, as you'd ever seen.

"Ms. Suzy, I need to use your phone, if I could, something's come up and I can't use ours, I sure would be grateful."

"Why, sure you can child, you can use the one in my bedroom if you need some privacy."

"Thank you, Ms. Suzy," Lisa Marie told her.

"Now, you youngin's, c'mon with me. I believe we got some ice cold milk with fresh chocolate chip cookies around here somewhere.

Lisa Marie's hands were trembling as she dialed the New York number of Harry Wellman, trying to remember what all she was supposed to tell him. The phone began to ring on the other end. "Hello," said the voice of Harry Wellman.

"Harry this is …" she began to say, but was cut short before she could give her name.

"I know it's you, Sarah, look, I understand you're upset about your brother and all the money he's been spending. But remember, rainy day's soon get better, oh and by the way, the address you wanted earlier is twenty one fifty seven, not twenty one fifty. I have to go now, but you stay there until it stop's raining, okay?" And then he hung up, he hoped that he had played that right and that Lisa would stay where she was at for at least the amount of time it took him to get down to the pay phone to return her call. Harry Wellman, was no fool, he didn't know how careful Joe had been but he himself, would take all precautions.

Ten minutes later, after retrieving the number from his Caller I.D., Harry Wellman, pushed the numbers into the payphone, after giving his billing number, the telephone began to ring on the other end.

"Hello?" He heard Lisa's voice.

"Okay, it's me, so let's make this quick, what kind of trouble is Joseph in?"

"He's in pretty deep, somebody's been blackmailing him in to not letting some of the horses he rides win, by threatening to hurt someone in the family, now the F.B.I. is involved and Joe's mother, has come up missing. Joe, is on the run and Harry, I have no idea what to do, I'm here in Rapid City with the kids, and I'm sure the F.B.I., is watching every move I make."

"Okay, listen real close, the reason they are sticking to you is because you're their link to Joe, now what are they trying to arrest him for exactly, or do you know?"

"I think conspiracy, fraud. Hell, I'm not sure what all."

"Okay, he told me to tell you like I did earlier. I'm only telling you again to be sure we're clear. It's a rainy day and the number is twenty one fifty seven, does that mean anything to you?"

"I think so, I'll have to check something out, and then let you know," said Lisa Marie, remembering what her and Joe, had talked about every time they moved to a new town.

"What I need to know from you is this, do you want me to represent him in this matter? If so, my suggestion is, that the three of you board a plane tomorrow morning, headed here to New York, once you get here, someone, more than likely myself, will come to pick you up."

"That sounds good to me, I don't want to stay here when I know where my husband's headed, and yes, I want you to represent him."

"When you get here, call me, now we better end the call."

"One more thing, why are you helping us like this? We don't have the money anymore for fees like yours."

"Let me tell you something, I never lost faith in that husband of yours, he's the best damn rider I've ever seen and besides that, he made me a hell'ava lot of money, I'm just giving some of it back! Now, I gotta go." Click, and the line was dead.

Lisa knew exactly what a rainy day meant and she also knew, that twenty one fifty seven, was actually a combination 21-50-07. The combination, Joe had kept to himself, which was to the floor safe in their bedroom closet, she didn't want to know the combo until she needed to, she had thought it ridiculous when Joe had it installed in every new place they moved to, and besides, she didn't like being part of his drug paranoia, but now it seemed that it was perfectly warranted, a rainy day meant, it was time to open it.

Joe and Chris had just taken off from the municipal airport, outside of Denver, on the south side, near Littleton. It was now dark outside as the two flew toward their next stop for fuel. They had talked about the dilemma that Joe was in, on the ride from Buffalo, but now, that they were again air born, they had grown quite, each lost in their own thoughts.

Joe had slipped back in time, to nineteen seventy two, the night that Lisa's dad had died. There was something that didn't make sense but he couldn't put his finger on it. He had kept it a secret from everyone that he knew, that it had not been a robbery, and that it had something to do with fixing races, or so he thought, something he had heard later, just didn't match up. What in the hell was it? That was his last thought as he dozed off. Joseph Leblanc had, had all he could stand for one day.

Agent Russo, himself, had boarded a commercial flight out of Rapid City, headed for Baton Rouge, Louisiana, from there, he would take a bureau helicopter to Carrencro. He was to meet with Charlie Leblanc, Joe's father, at the Leblanc farm, where Maggie, had last been seen by Charlie, before he went to feed his horses, stabled at Cajun Downs. When he had returned, his wife, was no-where to be found, her Monte Carlo was also gone, making Charlie think that maybe she ran to the store, or maybe, she also had gone to the track, to check on the tack shop that she still owned after buying Tracy out, some years back, and that he had just missed her somehow. However when she'd been gone for over an hour after he returned, he began to worry, so he had called the tack shop talking with Stephanie, which was the girl that ran the shop, but she had said that Mrs. Leblanc had not been in all day, now he was really starting to worry. And that's about the time that the F.B.I. came knocking, to let him know that something was a foul and that his son, was mixed up in it somehow or another. All Charlie knew for sure was, he was scared for his wife, and that some big shot agent was coming to talk with him in the morning. Meanwhile, there were agent's all over his house with all kinds of electrical wires hooked up to his telephone. He himself, just stared at the phone praying that his wife would call, and thinking, what in the hell have you done now, Joseph?

As he thought of his son, ole Charlie Leblanc, also let his mind slip back in time to when he was so proud of his son, he could have burst wide open.

Joe had only ridden for twenty eight day's at Cajun Downs, when he was sixteen but in those first day's of his career, Joe had won eighteen races, he had then received a call from an agent in New York, saying that Joe, should come try his luck in the Big Apple. Two day's later, he had boarded an airplane and within four months, Joe, had jumped to the leading apprentice in the nation in money earned, he had won the eclipse award for best apprentice, he won twelve major stakes races that year. It had seemed that Joseph Leblanc, was unstoppable. And then just a few short year's later, he had bottomed out. How could such a good kid with all the talent in the world have everything going his way and then bam, it was all gone. That just didn't add up in Charlie's mind. But maybe some answers were coming his way, however, the only answer he wanted, was to know where in the hell his wife was at, and that she was safe.

Lisa Marie and the children had left Suzy's house and were now at home. Lisa had explained a little of what was happening to Suzy and had asked her if she could feed their dog Boo-Boo, while they were out of town. Which Suzy had agreed to.

Lisa was now in the walk-in closet of her and Joe's bedroom, the children were asleep in their rooms, God, she thought, those kids have been through a lot today. Her hand's numbly worked the tumblers of the safe, click, there it was, she opened it slowly, not knowing what she might find. At first, she saw a money bag which she opened, it contained several bundles of one hundred dollar bills, there was also an envelope, that to she opened, to find a letter to her from Joe, and it read as follows:

Dear Lisa Marie, my soul mate for life: First, I want you to know just how much I love you, words written, can no way express my feeling for you. I know that if you are reading this, then something had either happened to me or—that part is not really important, what is however, will unfold before your eyes as you read on.

Most people, believe that my down fall started the day that I got my father's horse beat in New Orleans, even though I received the call just that morning, telling me not to finish anywhere near the front end, if not for the caller's next statement, I may have let the colt run anyway, however what I was told next, stopped me in my tracks. Lisa, I was told that your father's murder, was not just a robbery but an action taken against him, for winning the stake race, that night at Vinton Downs, and that, if I didn't do as I was told, then I could expect the same thing he had gotten only it would be someone that I held dear to my heart. Well, that could have meant you, or my parents, hell even Lannett, I didn't know just how serious they were and I was not willing to take any chances, if that meant throwing the race, then that's what I would do. And so I, did not let the horse run that day. My life has forever been changed, my father, and my mother, have been hurt deeply by my actions, but I would rather have them alive and safe, than the alternative I have been faced with. You Lisa, have been what has kept me going all these year's, you and the children, think not that killing myself has crossed my mind at times, but there is no way I could purposely let you face the future alone. Now, there are two reasons you could be reading this, let's go with the one that I am in favor of, which is not being dead. But that I have decided to take the bull by the horns and find out who is behind all of this, in doing so I firmly believe I will have to search the past, namely the last Saturday before Christmas nineteen seventy two. I imagine, that no matter where we are living, when you read this, your next move, should be to either go to Carrencro, to my parent's house or to New Orleans, with your mom. At any rate, I will be in touch, there should be enough money here to see you through until we can be together again. I love you and the children very much. Now, if I have past on, then you are to contact my father, and give him this letter so that he and my mother may know that in their son, there was some good after all.

Love always,
Joseph Greaden Leblanc

Tears were running down Lisa Marie's cheeks, she could not believe that her husband, the man, she had loved, ever since he had been just a boy, had kept all of this in. He had sacrificed his sanity and his very life, to protect the people, whom he dearly loved.

She knew that he loved his mom and dad, they had been so close, when he was younger, oh, how it must have been tearing him apart from the inside out.

That night, she fell asleep in their bed, clutching the tee shirt that Joe had worn the night before, trying to find comfort in his scent. Her last thought before she drifted off was of Joe and her making love just that morning and how sweet it had been.

Joe and Chris had flown into Rayne, Louisiana at just abut midnight, both were worn out, even though Joe had slept some of the way he was mentally drained.

Rayne, is a medium sized town, just southwest about thirty miles from Carrencro, the two men had checked into the Journey's End motel next to the tiny airport under Chris Johnson's name. Chris himself would fly out to San Antonio, come daylight, while Joe would have to decide what course of action to take. First he would have to get some kind of vehicle to take to Carrencro, if that's where he needed to go, hell, he wasn't sure of what he needed to do. He had not thought this through very well, and he sure wasn't Mickey Spillane or Dick Tracy.

He knew that the F.B.I. was in Carrencro, but somehow he needed to get in touch with his father, if he would even talk with him. Joe had missed the relationship that he had had with his parents, he and his dad had been really close. These thoughts took Joseph back into the past once again. He was remembering the first time that his father, let him ride in one of the match races, over at the non pari-mutual match track at Sunset, Louisiana which was about fifteen minutes from their small farm. He had been going to the different match track's in southern Louisiana, just about every Sunday afternoon with his parent's for a long time, and how he begged his dad to let him ride, but Charlie, even though he had put on about twenty pounds or so since he had retired, always rode his own horses at the matches. And rarely got beat, there was always somebody wanting his dad to ride their horses also, but he always declined. Charlie kept telling the young Joseph, that he'd get his chance, just give it time. And then that Sunday afternoon came that Joe did get his chance, he had been galloping horses on their little farm and helping his dad break the younger horses for about a year or so, he was now eleven years old. Charlie, Maggie, Lisa Marie, and Tracy along with Joe, had all gone to the match races in Sunset. Joe's dad, had taken and loaded a little sorrel gelding, and a bay mare, that stood about fifteen hands tall, in their two horse trailer and headed off for the races, with Joe and Lisa riding in the back of the pick-up truck. Joe had no idea that he was on his way, to make his match track debut. When they had gotten to the track, they unloaded the horses, then Charlie gave Joe a twenty dollar bill with two entry cards to take over to the entry booth. Back in those day's, you could bet between each other as much as you wanted, and you could enter your horses and run them as many times as you wanted to, however you were going to pay ten dollars, per horse, per race, no matter what. When he and Lisa got to the entry booth, Ms. Guidry was there to take the money and the entry slips, and as Joe handed them to her she looked at the slips then looked at Joe and again back at the slips, "Joe Leblanc, how old are you now?" She had asked, "I just turned eleven last month Ms. Guidry," he returned proudly.

"Well, either your daddy, made a mistake or you need to go take this consent form over for him to sign and then bring it back."

"What kind of consent form?" Joe asked, and then added, "You never gave us one before!"

"That's true young man, but if you're going to ride at this track, then your mama, or your daddy's, gonna sign one of these forms!"

Joe had just about jumped out of his skin, for his dad, had named Joseph Leblanc, as the jockey, of both horses on the entry slips.

Joe had remembered how happy he was that day, he was going to be one of the jockey's and he also had the prettiest girl in Louisiana, with him.

In his first race, he would ride the bay mare going three hundred yards, and she was wicked fast. Charlie had told his son, "Now Tee Joe, when they all load, you can't wait around and get tied on, you gotta be ready, it ain't like at the farm, this mare, she gonna win, you

```
------------------------------------------
Ector County Sheriff        L A W    E N F
TSG, INC.                           MEA
                                    Faci
------------------------------------------

Jail ID SO...... Inmate's Name........

  297260      90589 POWELL, HAROLD DWAINE


  298834      51037 REYES, ALFONSO JAVIER

  295060      65008 ROBERTSON, GEORGE
                    JERRAY JR.

  296673      96047 ROBIN, JESSE JEROME

  297890      65179 RUSSELL, RICHARD
                    ARTHUR

  294066      22391 WHIRLEY, DENNIS JACK,
                    SR
```

~~WWW.Live~~

WWW.LVTRIKES.COM

WWW1

WWW.TAILGUNNEREXHAUST.COM

WWW.3RIDE4YOU.COM

WWW.THOROUGHBRED.MOTORSPORTS.COM

WWW.bosshoss.com

just grab a handful-a-mane and hang on, that's all you gotta do boy, you hear?"

"Yes sir, Daddy, I hear."

And then Charlie, had legged his son into the saddle, and then climbed on a lead horse that he had borrowed, knowing full well that Little Joe was going to need help, getting the hopped up mare to the outdated starting gate.

Joe could still remember how proud he was sitting on top of that mare, what was her name? He thought back, trying to remember. "Lazy Liz", he said softly to himself. Well, there wasn't anything lazy about her, that was for sure.

"Now Joe, this mare, she gonna be a runnin' like hell, chasein' a drunkard, you just hunker down and don't mess with her son. She's alright now, you just hang-on." Charlie told his son. Looking back remembering that day, Joe realized that his father, was nervous and maybe a little scared for his son. Joseph, almost thirty years later was finding comfort in that, knowing that his dad really did love him.

Charlie dismounted behind the gate, he himself would handle the mare for Joseph in the starting gate to make damn sure his boy, gotta good clean break. Also, a lot of wrecks happen in the steel monster, prior to the race. Charlie Leblanc wanted and could be there for his son, when and if he needed him!

The mare had gotten antsy waiting in her slot for the last two to load, it would be a four horse match, the mare rared a couple of times pretty hard, rattle'n Joe just a little, but Charlie was right there saying, "easy son-easy, I got'cha, you tied on? Get ready!!!"

And then he heard from somebody else.

"All locked up!"

Bam!! The gates flew open, and the mare, by the third jump, was full throttle, and carrying Tee Joe at a rapid pace, down the lane, toward the finish line. He had won by a good half a length. He was now still full throttle around the turn, he couldn't get her stopped, down the backside they went, Joe was getting scared, the more he pulled on the reins, the faster she wanted to go, and then Joe looked up and there his dad was, Charlie, was waiting on the lead horse to catch his son, and when she was almost to him, he kicked his horse into gear matching the stride's of the mare as he reached out and took hold of the inside rein, he started slowing the mare down until they were back in front of the small grandstand, which was little more than some bleachers.

Joe had been out-of breath and so glad his dad, had been there to help him.

"Joseph, you win your first race!" His dad told him with a huge smile! Thinking back to that day and how scared he was, when he couldn't get the mare stopped, also made him realize that up until that one awful day in New Orleans, his dad had always been there for him. He thought now how scared his father must be for his mother. Joseph knew, that he, must now be there for his dad. He just didn't know how to go about it. He, that day, had also lost his first race, the gelding had gotten beat. Charlie had told his son, "Don't worry Joe, you always gotta take a little of the bad with the good, there will always be more losses's than wins, it's what you learn from them."

Joe felt like he was in a run away race now, one that he couldn't afford to lose. These were his thought's as he drifted off to sleep.

Lisa Marie had been awakened by her son as he crawled up on her bed. "Mama, what's going to happen to Daddy?" he asked.

As she looked into Bradly's eyes, she could see Joe when he had been just a boy himself. The memory of those day's past, made her miss her husband, even more.

"He's going to be just fine, Bradly." And as she hugged him, she said a prayer for Joe and Ms. Maggie.

"Okay now, Brad, we have a lot to do. You going to help me, right?" she asked as she looked into his eyes again.

"Yes, Mom, what do we have to do?"

"Well, first, I need you to go wake your sister, and tell her to come here, and then I want you to take a shower. We have to catch a flight to New York, this morning," she said this as she reached for the telephone. "Now hurry along and make sure to wash behind your ears, and brush your teeth," Lisa added.

"Lanette, get up!" Bradly hollered, as he hurried out of the room."

"We're going on a trip!"

Lisa sat holding the phone contemplating the call she knew she was going to make, as she dialed the number she took a deep breath and then listened as the phone rang on the other end.

"Hello," the voice said.

Lisa was frozen, she couldn't make her mouth move. She had not heard this voice, in such a long time.

"Hello, who is this?" the voice rising into the transmitter said.

"Charlie," Lisa said nervously.

"Yeah, this is Charlie Leblanc, who in the hell is this?

"Charlie, it's me, Lisa Marie."

Charlie's heart seem to melt at the sound of Lisa's voice.

"Lord, have mercy, where are you at, and where's my Joe?"

"I don't know, but I have a strong feeling he's heading your way," she answered as Lanett, came into the bedroom.

"Mom, where are we going," she asked, not realizing at first, that her mother was on the telephone. "Oh, I'm sorry, Mom."

"Charlie, hang on one second," Lisa said into the phone.

"Baby, I'll tell you after I get off the phone, now I need you to pack some things for you and Bradly, pack enough for at least three or four day's."

"I'm sorry, Charlie," Lisa Marie said once again into the telephone.

"It's okay, Lisa, now tell me, what in the hell has Joseph got us into now? You know my wife is missing and the F.B.I. is crawling all over down here!"

"I know, look Charlie, I don't know what it's about other than some kind of race fixing scam..."

"I knew it, why can't he stay straight, now he's went and put us right in the middle of it!" Charlie blurted, cutting off Lisa, from finishing her sentence.

"Charlie, it's not how it look's, Joe was being blackmailed all these years, look, I can't explain it right now; have you heard anything from or about Maggie?"

"No, not a word Lisa, some guy with the FBI, some agent named Russo, is supposed to meet here with the rest of his cronies, to try and explain what's going on, he should be here around nine a.m., what is it now? About eight thirty?"

"Yeah Charlie, it's exactly seven thirty here in Rapid City, so it's eight thirty there. I know this is hard on you, I wish there was something I could say, to make it easier but I can't. I will tell you this though and you need to listen, Joseph love's you very much, he didn't have option's, when he did what he did. He saved some people that he cared deeply for in the process, well, he just damned near destroyed himself. Whether you want to believe it or not isn't the point."

"Are you telling me that somebody was threatening my son, into not letting horses win, that were supposed to?"

"That's exactly what I'm telling you Charlie, I have no idea who, however, it stands to reason, that whoever has Maggie, is the one that has dictated Joe's life and ours for a very long time."

"Lisa,do you think Maggie's alive?"

"I pray that she is Charlie, that's all we can do," Lisa said as optimistically as she could.

"Where do you think Joe is?" Charlie asked.

"I don't know, I just don't know," she returned.

"What are you and the kids going to do? As a matter of fact, how are my grandchildren?" Charlie asked feeling extremely old.

"There good, Charlie, there great kids. I can't believe that you have deprived yourself of them all these years. Surely you had to know that Joe...well, you had to know, that he had his reason's." Lisa said this as a single tear rolled down her cheek. "Charlie, I have to go, I have to find my husband, to try and help him. He's looking for his mother and he needs our help!" Lisa Marie gently laid the phone in it's cradle, she needed to let Charlie dwell on what she had told him, and also she had to get it in gear. Reaching for the directory she called out, Bradly, are you out of the shower?

"Yes ma'am, I'm packing a suitcase, Lanett's in the bathroom now," her son answered.

Lisa, was so proud of her children, they knew how to pull together and get things done. She hoped that the rest of the family, would do the same thing, meaning Joe and his father.

Dialing the number, she had found, she listened, as it rang once, twice, three...

"Hello, Northwest Airlines, how may I help you?"

"Yes ma'am, when's your next flight to New Orleans, Louisiana?"

"Let me see, that would be one-forty this afternoon, would you like to make a reservation?"

"Yes I would, for three, first class, the name is Leblanc."

As Lisa, finished making the flight reservations, she then hung up the receiver and thought to herself, I hope

I'm doing the right thing, not going to New York.

Daylight had leaked in through the curtains of the Journey's End Motel. Chris Johnson was just opening his eyes. "What time is it?" the cowboy asked, as he yawned.

"Eight o'clock, time to get a move on for me, my friend," Joe answered.

"You take a shower yet, Joe?"

"No, not yet, I was just going to though unless you want to go first."

"Nah, go ahead," Chris said.

And with that, Joseph, went into the bathroom. As he let the hot water run down his back, he was thinking of what he should do. He was also hoping that his mother was still alive. What he didn't know was, what these people, stood to gain by killing her. As a matter of fact, he himself, was no longer any use, to whoever this Headless Horseman, had been all of these years. What kind of game were they playing?

Maybe, though, they were holding his mother, for a ransom, but he didn't know how much good that would do, for he didn't have what some would call a lot of money, and most of what he had, nobody knew about anyway. It seemed to Joe, that the more he thought it through, the more confused he became. Surely, this had to be about something other than fixing races, and money, but what? What in the hell did they want? Why hadn't he questioned, this whole thing a lot more when it got started, is the question he now asked himself for which he had no answer.

He was also trying to remember what had plagued his mind about the night that Gerard, had been killed. There was definitely something there, but what, he just couldn't put his finger on it. Drying off and then pulling on his jeans, he came out of the bathroom.

"Hey, Joe, do you feel like going next door to the station and get us some coffee?" Chris asked, digging in his pocket for some money. "Also, I need a pack of Marlboro," he added.

"No, not at all," he returned saying, "put your money away, I got this,"

"Thanks," Chris said as he headed for the shower.

The Louisiana mornings, was something that Joe had missed, maybe it was being close to the water, or just the smell. He wasn't sure. He wished that better circumstances had brought him back but they hadn't and cold reality of that, was enough to chill him to the bone, even on a July morning, in southern Louisiana. Walking into the shell station, he made his way back to the coffee pot, poured a large cup, then gathered up some sugars and creamers for Chris and he then decided on a cold soda pop for himself, he pulled a Dr. Pepper from the cold case and went to the register.

"Is that all," said the cashier.

"I need a pack of Marlboro, also," Joe told the little old woman. As she handed the cigarettes to Joe, she said, "don't you know these things are bad for you." It was just like somebody in Louisiana, to tell you what was on their minds.

"I know they are, but they are for somebody else ma'am," Joe said, and then just like that, it hit him like a rock, when he and Lisa, were still just kids, they had tried smoking a cigarette that Lisa had gotten from a friend of hers, however, about the same time, they had realized that they weren't going to be smokers, Lisa's mom, Tracy, had busted them when she came behind the tack trailer that she and Joe's mom ran.

"What in the world are y'all doin'?" Tracy had exclaimed

"Uh-uh we…" Joe had been unable to get his mouth to workin'.

"Well, the way y'all are about to choke, and Lisa, your daddy despised cigarettes."

That's what was now banging on Joe's mind, all those years ago, Gerard had gone to the foodmart for something which Joe couldn't remember anybody saying what for, however, the clerk had said, that he remembered Gerard buying a Dr. Pepper and a pack of Marlboro's just like Joe had just done, if Gerard didn't smoke and neither did Tracy, then who was Gerard buying those cigarettes for at one o-clock in the morning?

"Young man, are you alright?" asked the cashier, bringing Joe back to the present. "You look like you've just seen a ghost," she added with a concerned look on her face.

"Yes, ma'am, I think I just heard from a ghost, but I'm getting better," he stated, as he turned, walking out of the station, leaving the older woman to contemplate what Joseph had said.

Walking back to the motel room thinking over what he had just realized, out of the corner of his eye he noticed a dark blue Suburban with tinted windows. He wasn't for sure if it was the F.B.I. but if it wasn't, whoever it was, well, they were missing a damn good chance! At any rate Joe wasn't taking any chances, so ducking back behind a van, he double-back toward the pay phone, outside of the Shell station. Pulling some change from his pocket along with the motel key that had the telephone number on it, he pushed in the required thirty five cents and dialed the motel lobby.

"Hello, Journey's End Motel."

"Yeah, room one twenty seven please," Joe said

"Hello," Chris said, answering the phone, on the second ring.

"Chris, I think you're fixing to have company, it's the F.B.I., tell 'em whatever you want but I gotta go, man I'm sorry about this."

"Joe, you just find your mom, I'll handle this here, good luck partner." And then without another word, he set the phone down and went to answer the door that was now being pounded on.

Joseph had seen the two agents get out of the suburban and as they knocked on the door of the room that was occupied by his good friend, Joe slipped around the corner of the station to see a truck driver, headed toward his semi.

"Excuse me, you wouldn't be headed down the road toward Carrencro, would you?" Joe asked the trucker as he caught up with him.

"Sure would friend, going up to Oppalousas, you need a ride?"

"I sure do mister, I surely do," Joe said

Charlie, was sitting at his kitchen table just staring at the telephone, only minutes after his daughter-in law Lisa had hung up the phone. It rang again, the agent, operating the trace machine waited for one ring, then two, he then gave the okay sign for Charlie to answer it. "Hello," he said, somewhat nervously.

"Don't talk, just listen. I have your wife, and the time being she is safe, she will not stay that way if you do not do exactly as I say. It is now eight-forty-fine, I will call again in one hour with instructions." The caller had ended the call, not giving the F.B.I. enough time to trace the call.

Charlie, sat there completely out of tune with what was going on around him, the only thing he could think, was, that this was crazy. It was like something out of a movie, and a bad one at that.

"Mr. Leblanc," a voice said, bringing Charlie back from his thoughts.

"Yeah," he returned, as he looked up.

"Mr. Leblanc, this is Agent Russo, he's the one I told you about that had contact with your son, yesterday.

"Hello, Mr. Leblanc, nice to meet you," Russo said as he extended his hand.

Charlie, did not offer his hand, as he said, "Sit down, Mr. Russo. Me and you, we gonna have us a good ol' fashion Cajun sit down and what we call, a come to Jesus meetin'."

Sitting down in the chair, that was offered to Agent Russo, he started, "Mr. Leblanc, look, I know how you …" but was cut short. "No, you don't know a damn thing about the way I feel, you say something stupid like that again, I'm gonna knock hell out'a you, now you just listen!" Charlie told the agent in an agitated tone, his Cajun anger was just about to boil over. "There's two thing's going to happen right now, first, your going to tell me exactly what you believe, my son, has done, and then you are going to sit, right here with me, so that when these people, that have my wife, call back in less than an hour, you can try one more time to trace the call! If you don't get it done this time, you're going to pack up all this garbage and get the hell off my land, are we clear on that?"

"Mr. Leblanc, you're going to have to give us time, besides, this is a federal investigation. You don't have a lot to say about it at this point, we've taken total jurisdiction in this matter. Hell, the local sheriff hasn't even been notified."

Charlie had gotten up from the table, holding his coffee cup, he looked into the eyes of Agent Russo as he said, "My friend, you got one more chance, and then, as they say, in my world, all bets are off."

Both men said nothing, each studying the other when Russo's cell phone sounded. Taking the phone from his belt he answered. "Hello, Russo here."

As Russo listened intently to the person on the other end, Charlie looked at the clock on the kitchen wall, it read nine-forty. Just five minutes more and the call should come in, Charlie thought. God, he hoped that Maggie was safe, he couldn't even imagine how he would handle it, if anything were to happen to her. She had been his whole life, her and Joe.

As Charlie, reflected back on the last twelve years, a tear rolled down his cheek, could Lisa Marie be right about Joe being blackmailed into not letting his horse win that big race in New Orleans, all those years ago, and if so…well, Charlie couldn't imagine what his son had been subjected to. He was angry at whoever was behind this, but he was really pissed at himself for not believing better of his only son.

After speaking briefly into his phone, Russo replaced it into the holster attached to his belt. "Well, Mr. Leblanc, your son Joseph, is here in Louisiana, as a matter of fact he just got into a tractor trailer rig with a truck driver and it appears that they are headed in this direction."

"How do you know for sure where Joseph's at? You been following him?"

"We've had him in our sights pretty much since he flew out of Buffalo, South Dakota in a small plane with a cowboy, named Chris Johnson. We were just about to take him into custody this morning at a motel over in Rayne, but somehow he was next door at the station getting coffee when my agents went to the room after finding out that only Mr. Johnson was in the room, they then caught sight of Joseph, in this eighteen wheeler.

The agents wanted to know what they should do. We've decided to follow him a while longer.

At that moment, the Leblanc's house phone, began ringing. Charlie reached for it, Russo touched his hand as he said, "Mr. Leblanc, please keep your cool and keep them, on the line for as long as you can..."

Charlie, nodded, that he understood and then picked up the receiver on the third ring. "Hello," he said, hesitantly.

"First, I know that the F.B.I. is there, they have to leave, secondly your son, is in Louisiana, you need to locate him, it will take both of you to save your wife..." The caller had hung up.

"Enough time or what?" Russo snapped.

"I believe so boss, still pinpointing, it's a trac phone and the signal is coming out of Baton Rouge, and it appears to be on the move."

Lisa Marie, had just gotten off of the telephone with the lawyer, in New York, telling him that she was not coming to the big apple, instead she was going to her mother's, in New Orleans. She wanted him to give Joe, that message if he called.

Lisa had talked with Tracy earlier, her mother, was clearly upset at the new's of Maggie's kidnaping.

She had told Lisa, that she thought it was a good idea to head toward Carrencro, to support Charlie, during this crisis. Lisa, in return had said, that they could make up their minds about that once she and the children got there.

Lisa had finished packing, everyone had taken their showers. They were ready, the only thing Lisa was waiting around for was in hopes that Joe would call before they had to leave for the airport.

As she waited, her thoughts, roamed back to the fact, that she hated going back to New Orleans, and very rarely did. The memories of her father, were sometimes more than she could bare. However, her mother had moved to New Orleans, after marrying jockey agent Brian Gunn, about a year after Lisa's own wedding. Brian was alright, she supposed, although he never seemed to have any real money making jock's.

Back in Carrencro, Joe Leblanc had the trucker pull into the Win, Place, and Show. Which was a hole in the wall bar, about a quarter of a mile past Cajun Downs. The bar itself had changed owners many times through the years but it's physical makeup had stayed the same, for as long back as Joe could remember.

After thanking the truck driver for the lift, he climbed down from the rig and watched the semi pull back onto the highway.

Joseph, was not aware of the Federal agents that were watching from a distance.

As he took in the view of Cajun Down's racing oval he said, softly to himself. "God, it's good to be home."

The bar, had been a favorite of stable area employee's, such as exercise riders, grooms, even some trainers and jockey's. They would stop in for a beer or drink, after the morning chores were done. Joe's dad, would stop in from time to time, to catch up, on the latest talk around town.

As Joe stepped through the door into the coolness of the dimly lit room, few heads turned, as the patrons were more interested in their beer and conversations.

He looked around to see if he recognized anyone, even though it had been a long time since he had been in these parts, it was still a race track community and you never knew who you might run into.

Pulling himself onto a barstool, the bar maid, a pretty dark haired girl, about twenty-five, asked, "What can I get'cha?"

He didn't want a beer but just so he wouldn't look out of place he said, "I'll take a Bud Light."

"Sure thing," she returned, reaching into the cooler, she pulled out a bottle of beer and set it on the bar, "if you need anything else, my names Brandi."

"Thanks, Brandi."

"No problem," she answered, smiling, as she moved down the bar to take another order.

On the wall, behind the bar, were a lot of win pictures, taken at Cajun Downs, as well as other tracks, across the country.

In the middle of these pictures was a blown up one, of a sixteen year old kid, named Joe Leblanc, on his first winner. Where they had gotten it, Joe had no idea. Next to it though was another win picture of Joe, winning the Derby, in Kentucky, those were good times, back then. Money, flowed, almost like water.

Joe remembered how, that in December's past, he and Lisa Marie, before the children came along, would take off and go, wherever they wanted, at that time, in his career, the sky was the limit.

Looking below the pictures of himself, brought him back to the reality of it all. The newspaper clipping that was posted to the wall read, "Top rider, get's favorite beat, on the Derby road, in New Orleans," the clipping next to that one stated, "Charlie Leblanc, loses Derby contender, due to questionable ride, by Joseph Leblanc." Joe could see a smaller article, that read: "Probe by Stewards, declares Leblanc, not at fault." Joe was thinking, what a lie. The track, just didn't want bad publicity, and so it had been swept under the carpet, similar to the way, Joe's career had been.

The two agents that were watching the bar entrance, from across the highway, made a phone call, to Russo. "Mr. Leblanc, that was the agents, that have been following your son. They say, that he is at some bar, called the Win, Place and Show next to…"

"I know where it is Russo," Charlie said, interrupting the agent, and then adding, "I'm going to get my son, and I can only ask, that you don't arrest him. You know what the maniac, Headless Horseman wants, he wants you gone."

"Look, Mr. Leblanc, I'm on your side, no matter what you think. I'm not going to arrest Joe, just yet, I'm willing to see where this thing goes. We'll be gone when you guy's get back but we'll be close."

"Thank you, Mr. Russo, now I've got to go."

"One more thing, Leblanc."

"What's that?"

"Good luck, and I mean that sir," Russo said, sincerely.

"I know you do, Russo, I know you do," Charlie responded, as he walked out of his kitchen.

Russo shook his head at the determined old Cajun, as he turned to the other agents, "What about that trace, do anymore good?"

The trace and pinpoint man, spoke up. "We found the phone alright, in a trash can, in Denim Springs."

"Damn, there's no telling how many of those damn thing's they have."

"Well, let's pack up and make it quick, we're setting up shop at the Evangeline Motel, across the highway from the race track."

Charlie pulled into the parking lot of the Win, Place and Show, he didn't go unnoticed by the federal agents nor by the gentleman in the burgundy Chrysler, who at the sight of Charlie Leblanc, punched in a number on his cell phone, after three rings, it was answered on the other end. "Yeah?"

"Daddy rabbit, is about to meet Peter Cottontail," said the Chrysler man.

"Gotcha," the other man replied, then ended the call.

Brandi asked Joe, "So you know my name. Now what's yours?"

Joe hesitated, he wasn't sure if he was among friends or not.

"Don't be ashamed son, tell 'em who you are," Charlie said.

The folks in the bar, had not paid attention to Charlie when he had walked in, however they were all ears now. They knew who Charlie was, for sure, and now, they had a pretty good idea who the newcomer was at the bar.

"Hello, Dad," Joe said, turning around. You could hear people saying, under their breath and among each other, "Is that Tee Joe? Well, I'll be damned, I can't believe it."

"Sa va mi, Tee Joe?" Charlie asked, closing the distance between them, tears starting to run down his cheeks. The tough old Cajun's heart, was melting.

"Bein bein, an twa, Papa? Joe replied, and asked how his father was, as he did, he came off of the bar stool and met his dad, father and son embraced, for the first time, in a very long time. As they did, Charlie said, "I'm not good, Joe, I'm not good at all. They have your mother."

"I know, Dad, but we're gonna get her back, I promise," Joseph told his father as they both looked at each other.

"Joe, we have to go, the people that have her, are going to call the house. When they called last, they said,that it would take both of us to get Maggie back."

"Dad, how did you know I was here?"

"The F.B.I. has had you pegged, ever since you flew, out of South Dakota."

Everyone in the bar had turned back around letting the two Leblanc's have their reunion. Most people knew the story of Joe and his dad. Right now, they were smart enough to stay out of the way.

No one paid much attention when they left, or so it seemed, there would be lots of talk later though.

As Joe and Charlie drove back to the Leblanc farm, Joe took in the country that he had loved so much when he was growing up. They went past Arcenaux's Grocery, where he and Lisa Marie would ride their bicycles to after school for a peach flavored soda pop and those fresh cracklins that Ms. Ida would make. And there was the little field that they use to play softball in. While taking all of this in Joe was over taken by grief, he looked over at his dad and realized that Charlie Leblanc, somewhere along the way, had gotten old.

"Dad," he said, "I am so sorry for this, can you ever forgive me?" Charlie pulled the pick-up over to the side of the road and looked his son dead in the eye, "Joseph, Lisa Marie called me this morning and told me most of what she knew. I'm the one that should have known that something was wrong, and that you would never have done anything against your family. I rode races long enough, I should have known it in my heart." Charlie was telling these things to his son as he started to cry. "I'm sorry Joe, I should have been somebody, you could have come to, but I wasn't."

Joe wasn't sure what to say, "It's going to be alright, whatever it takes, we'll get Mom back."

And then ole Charlie said, "That's right son, we gotta be strong for her."

Pulling back onto the road home, Joe at least felt one huge burden lifted from his shoulders.

Meanwhile, a seven forty seven, was taxing into the terminal,at the New Orleans International Airport, carrying Lisa Marie and her two children.

Lisa's mother was there at the gate to meet them, it had been a few years since she had seen Tracy. But the two had no trouble spotting each other.

"Lisa Marie, my lord, you look good, and look at my grandkids! They have gotten so big."

"Hello, Mom," Lisa said as her mother wrapped her arms around her daughter.

"I have missed you so much darling," Tracy said, letting go and holding her arms open to her grand children.

"Are you my grandma?" Bradly asked.

"Yes, she is Brad, don't you remember her?" Lanett said, poking her brother.

"Ow! Quit it, Lanett."

"Both of you stop it," Lisa Marie said.

"Lanette, you're growing up so fast. Just look at you."

"Hello, Grandma," Lanette replied as Tracy gave her a hug.

"Let's get out of here, Mom, we need to pick up our bags and the kids and I are starving." And as they started down the corridor toward the baggage claim, Tracy took her daughter's hand and asked "Have you heard anything about Maggie?"

"Not a word, Mother. I did talk with Charlie. He sounded like he was coming apart at the seams."

"Well, I imagine he is, wouldn't you be, Lisa?"

"Mom, I am coming apart at the seams but I don't want to talk about it here."

Once they were in the car Lisa Marie asked, "Mom, how's Brian doing these day's?"

"Oh, he's doing okay. Right now, he's up in Bossier City, hustling book for Carlos Remerez and some bug rider. They aren't winning very many races, so money's a little tight right now," Tracy answered of her husband.

"Mom, I'm hungry," Lanette told her mother.

"Baby, we'll get something in a few minutes," Lisa answered, and then asked her mom, "Where can we stop to get something to go? I want to get to your house in case Joe calls, plus I think we should call Charlie and, Mom, you and I have some talking to do once the kids get fed."

"How about a bucket of chicken and some red beans and rice? Does that sound alright to y'all?" Tracy asked, glancing in the rear view mirror to check the reactions of her grandchildren.

"Sounds good to me. I'm so hungry I could eat an elephant!" Bradly answered.

"Me, too," added Lanette.

"Well then, I know just the place," Tracy offered, and then glancing over at her daughter she smiled and said, "Lisa, it's good to see y'all, I really mean that."

"I know, Mom, it's good to see you, too." Lisa's mind drifted off to a time in the past that had not been so pleasurable with her mother. But she sure as hell didn't want to go over that again.

After a short stop at Popeyes to pick up the chicken, they were now just around the corner from Tracy's, and as they pulled into the drive, a federal agent went past in a Pontiac Trans Am. And as he did, he made a call on his cell phone, which was answered on the second ring.

"Yeah, it's Conner, they just pulled into the driveway of a home on Laplace Drive." He then listened and said, "I got it, I'm on 'em like glue."

Once they were in the house, the kids at the kitchen table eating, Lisa Marie and her mother went into the living room. "Mom, sit down, we need to talk about some things that happened a long time ago." Lisa told her mother, as she herself took a seat on the sofa and patting the place beside her indicating she wanted her mother to sit next to her.

As Tracy sat down she noticed that her mother had been holding her age well, doing some quick calculations, Lisa figured her mother, would be sixty on her next birthday.

"Mom," she said, taking her hand in hers, "I've found out some things about Dad's murder, that I believe you should know."

"What on earth are you talking about Lisa?" Her mother asked, perplexed.

"Well, Joe's, being black..." Lisa was interrupted by the ringing of Tracy's telephone, and she thought at least for the moment, that she had been saved by the bell. Even though she needed to discuss these matters with her mother, it didn't make her like it any better.

"Hello," Tracy said, into the telephone.

While her mother seemed to go into a small conversation, Lisa got up to check on the children, and to give her mother a little privacy. After getting the kids some more milk and giving each a big hug she told them how much her and Joe loved them. She then returned to the living room, just about the time Tracy, was getting off of the phone. And as Lisa sat back down, her mother said, "That was Brian, he's thinking about taking that bug rider to San Antonio, for the race meet there. They just can't seem to get anything going in Bossier City. It's just to tough a meet there."

"Have you told him what's going on with Ms.Maggie, and Joe for that matter?" Lisa asked.

"No, I haven't really talked to him that much in the last couple of days, I did tell him that you all were coming for a visit. I have missed y'all so much. I just can't imagine why you've stayed gone for so long."

Lisa thought, but did not say aloud,

"You know damn well, why I've stayed gone."

"Look, Mom, let's talk…" But again she was interrupted, this time by her mother.

"Now; what kind of non-sense have you found out about your fathers death?"

"His murder, mother! He was murdered, don't you remember how they found him?" Lisa Marie was starting to get upset, something that she didn't need to do. She had to now be more cool and calm.

'Lisa, I know full well that your father, was murdered, what I don't know is, why you are dragging it back up after all these years. What good could come from it?"

"Because, Mom, the way they started blackmailing Joe, into stiffing races was with the threat that if he didn't do what they said to do, they would make sure that what had happened to Gerard, would happen to someone dear to Joe's heart. Are you understanding what I'm telling you? Whoever it was or is, wanted Dad to not let that horse win the stake at Vinton Downs, the night he was killed."

"That's insane Lisa, you and Joe have lost your mind!" Tracy said, raising her voice.

"Is that right Mom? You think so? Then I suppose Maggie's kidnaping, is a figment of our delusional minds!" Lisa snapped, and then taking a breath while trying to regain her composure, her mother got up and went to the bookcase, picked up a pack of cigarettes, then as she tapped one out of the pack, she said, "Lisa Marie, just suppose you're right about your father, who could be behind something like that and then keep it up for so long?" Tracy then picked up a lighter and as she started to light up Lisa spoke,

"Mom, when did you start smoking? You never smoked before, did you?"

"No, I didn't; I only started last year. I really don't know why I started except for from time to time I'd take a drag off of Brians and now, when I get upset or board it seems to help. But that's not important, what is though, is this ridiculous notion that your dad was murdered over some race fixing scam," Tracy told her daughter.

"Mom, why do you say it's so ridiculous? You know damn well that thing's like fixing races, and holding back winners to build the odds, happens all of the time. Even if you don't want to believe it, it's true! Ask Brian, I'll bet he can tell you, I'm sure," Lisa Marie was saying as the telephone began ringing, startling both women.

Tracy picked up on the third ring as she was stubbing out her half smoked cigarette. "Hello," she said.

"Hello, Tracy, it's Joe. Is my wife there?"

"Joseph, are you alright?" asked Tracy and then before he could answer, she also asked, "Where are you honey? You've got poor Lisa and the kids worried sick!"

"Mom, give me the phone!" Lisa said as she got up to move closer, and grabbing it from her mother, she

spoke into the telephone "Joseph, where in the hell are you?" Then not giving him a chance to answer, she asked, "Are you alright? God, I miss you!"

"Yes, Lisa, I'm okay, I'm at Dad's..." and then being interrupted, Lisa said, "Well, thank God for that, have you heard anything about Maggie?"

"We know or at least they have told Dad that she is safe for the time being, and as long as we follow their instructions she'll stay that way. We're waiting on them to call now. How are the kids? I love y'all so much! And I miss you guys!" Joe told his wife as he thought about, how much his family meant to him.

"Joseph, we're fine, the kids are good. We're coming to Carrencro, though!" She told her husband in a very determined voice.

"Lisa, I want y'all with me, that's for sure but I also want you safe. I don't know how safe you'd be here, besides Dad and I need to find out exactly what they want us to do. So please, just wait there and I'll call you back the minute we know our next move."

"Joseph, I know, but listen we…" She was interrupted by her husband as he said, "Lisa, I don't have time to argue this out, you'll just have to trust me on this. I'm doing the very best I can! I love y'all with all of my heart, I gotta go."

"Joe, we love you too, please be careful…" She returned, as the call was ended.

Lisa Marie setting the phone down, turned to see that Lanette and Bradly had come into the livingroom, with Lanette asking, "Was that Dad?"

As tears rolled down her cheeks she crossed the room to her children and as she took them into her arms, they all hugged one another in a family embrace, Lisa told them both, "Yes, that was your father, and he sends his love."

"Mom, is Dad going to be okay?" asked Bradly.

Lisa Marie squeezing them even more answered, "Yes, he is; however, he needs our prayers." With Lisa comforting her children, Tracy looked on, not really knowing what to do.

Meanwhile, over in Carrencro, Joe was sitting at the kitchen table with his father, waiting for the kidnapers to call.

"So, Joseph, let's go back to why you didn't let my horse run in New Orleans," Charlie said. "Maybe, we should take notes, there has to be some clue to who in the hell's behind this."

"Dad, you know how good, I was doing back then, I had the world by the tail. I had real good prospects that spring, for the stake races, I rode a colt in the Fantasy stake's, down in Hot Springs, we set a track record, then there was the Sportsmans Handicap, in Chicago, the list could go on and on and then that phone call came in, they said, throw the race or else someone I loved, was going to get hurt, I couldn't let that happen," Joseph told his father as he buried his face into his hands and adding. "And after they dominated my life all these years, I believed the F.B.I., when they said Mom was protected, and look what's happened."

"Joe, you did the best, you knew how." And as Charlie looked at his son, his thoughts went to a similar conversation that they had had at this very table.

It was the spring of nineteen seventy six, ole Speck Dubois had bought a Colt off Sonny Richard, he was a quarter horse that didn't stand over fourteen-two, but he was some kind of fast, going two hundred and twenty yards, well Speck, didn't train quarter horses, but he had bought the colt so his grandson Joe could have something nice and fast to ride in the Del Rio Futurity down in Texas. Since Joe, wasn't sixteen yet, he couldn't get a jock's license at the pari-mutual tracks. So he was still riding at all the match track's across the state when his grandfather heard about the futurity for two year olds.

Well, ole Speck doted on Joe pretty good and wanted him to get some exposure other than in Louisiana. So they hauled the colt down to south Texas for the futurity trials.

They had decided that if the colt ran good, and came back out of the race in good shape, then they would stay for the finals the next weekend.

Joe was real excited, there were some pretty good riders, that had come over from New Mexico. The futurity was at the time worth about ten thousand. Speck had paid about half that much for the horse with no guarantee that he would win anything. The thing though, was this, he loved watching his grandson having fun with the game.

Joe had drawn the three hole and when they opened the gate, that little quarter colt broke so damn hard that the ground broke out from behind him causing the colt to stumble, leaving there. By the time Joe got the colt to running it was to late, in quarter horse-racing there is no time for mishaps or mistakes, you have to be gone from jump. However, he had ran third, the bad news was that when he had stumbled, he had grabbed a quarter causing the toe grab on the back shoe to slice the heel of the front foot. It would take time to heel, and so even though they had qualified for the finals. They thought it to be in the better interest of the colt to save him for another day.

Once they were home, the next morning, Charlie had came into the kitchen and sitting at this same table was his son, Joseph. When Joe realized that his father had walked in, he looked up and said, "Dad, I'm really sorry, that I didn't do better on that colt."

Charlie had told his son, "Joseph, there was nothing you could do, you did the best you could do. Losses in horse racing, well, that's just part of it. We can only do so much and then we have to ride the tide. One thing for damn sure, you'll lose a lot more races than you'll ever win, so don't dwell on the losses, only enjoy the wins."

Charlie was remembering that conversation of so many years ago when the phone rang. Charlie reached for it, picking it up he said, "Hello."

"Well, so far so good," the voice on the other end said, and then adding, "Mr. Leblanc, I see you found Joseph, now we can start getting down to the real deal…" The caller was then interrupted by Charlie.

"Look, I want to talk with my wife. I want to know that she's alright…!"

"Are you finished, Mr. Leblanc? I hope so because one more outburst like that and this will happen"…the phone call had been ended.

"Dad, what happened? What did they say?" Joe asked.

As Charlie set the phone down, he said, "They hung up, damn, I've got to keep my cool, Joseph." And then the phone began ringing again. Answering it this time was Joe.

"Hello."

"Well, hello, Joe, don't be like your ole dad there, just listen. Between you and your father, you will pick a track for you to go ride at, one that you have not been to before, but one where people will ride you. I will call back tomorrow at this time."

"What about…" Joe started, but then realized that the Headless Horseman had ended the call.

"Joseph, what did he say? What are we supposed to do?" Charlie asked his son in an unstable voice.

"Dad, I don't know what they're up to, but it's looking like there just might be some more race fixing going on."

"What in the hell do you mean, Joseph?"

"Well, they want us to pick or find a racetrack that I have not been to before, where the trainers will ride me on their horses. We have until tomorrow to choose one."

"Son, that makes no sense, how are they going to profit from that?"

"I have no idea, I do know this though, we have to start calling agents that we know, that will be willing to hustle my book, know where we can start, Dad?"

"Son, I have no idea, I would imagine we first need to eliminate the tracks where you've ridden before, right?"

"Well, hand me that pen and paper and I'll start jotting down some places," Joe told his father, and then added, "Dad, you know most places, the trainers, they know me alright, and if they don't know me by sight, they sure know the name and it's not a good thing with a lot of people."

"Joe, this whole thing is crazy, what in the world do they want from us? This is total crap!"

"Yes, Dad, it is, I've been playing with these people for a long time. We don't have the luxury of another game, for us, it's the only one in town."

While both father and son worked on locating a racetrack that would serve the criteria of what the Headless Horseman wanted, Joe's wife and mother were having their own conversation in New Orleans.

"Mom, I'm telling you that Dad was killed over not throwing a race when he was suppose to, and you would rather believe it was over a robbery."

"No, Lisa, that's not what I'm saying, however this is my point, it does not matter how he died only that he did die, and no matter what crap you and Joseph drag up it's not going to change one damn thing!"

Tracy was lighting up another cigarette, blowing out the smoke, she continued. "And another thing, with Joseph's reputation, well he might be making the whole damn thing up as a cover up for his own gambling or drugs or God knows what for that matter!"

"That's it mother, you've said quite enough! You know there was a time when you thought that Joseph Leblanc hung the moon, but I guess that was when he was making the big money!" And without another word Lisa Marie stormed out of the living room and into the front yard, tears were streaming down her cheeks. Why was this happening to them? Life for Lisa Marie had been one big roller coaster ride. In the beginning of her life, her dad was a good jockey that made enough money to where they had lived very comfortable, her father had loved her so much and she had loved him. And then in the blink of an eye he was gone, murdered, life for her had taken a drastic turn. But then there was Joe, even when they were just kids, Joe had been there for her. He protected her, she felt safe.

Like the night that she had left the grandstand at Cajun Downs, walking back to the Leblanc's barn where Joe was cooling out one of his dad's horses after a race. She had been thirteen and Joe fifteen. Well, Ronny Deville was almost sixteen and he had cornered her as she came around the end of Arcenaux's barn, it was dark and he had scared her, he had smelled like he had been drinking whiskey or something,. He had grabbed her and tried to give her a kiss but she had broken free and started runnin, and then he was chasing her all the way to the Leblanc barn, he had been laughing and calling to her, "Come back, you little bitch!" By the time she got to where Joe was, she was out of breath and crying.

"Lisa Marie, what in the world's wrong? All that she had to do was say Ronny's name and Joe took off like he'd been shot out of a cannon. By the time she got to where Joe had found Ronny, there was already a small gathering around the two boy's, she could hear a couple of them saying, "I've got twenty on the Leblanc kid," he didn't get any takers though because Joe had made quick work of what he was doing which was beatin' the hell out of Ronny!

That fight had cost ole Charlie a smooth fifty, that's what the stewards fined him. But all Charlie had said was, "Joe, if that kid does something stupid like that again, I got another fifty so you beat hell out of him again, you hear." And then Charlie had winked at Lisa and said, "Now, that's how we do things."

Lisa Marie had known from that moment on that the Leblanc's, were very special people.

"Lisa, I'm sorry, honey. I know you're under a lot of strain with Joe and all," Tracy told her daughter as she came up behind her, touching Lisa's shoulder.

Lisa Marie turning around to face her mother said, "Mom, I'm sorry, too." The two women, mother and daughter hugged as Tracy said, "It's going to be alright, I'm sure of it."

Sniffling just a little, Lisa Marie answered, "I sure hope you're right. I also wish Joe would call. I want to be near him so bad."

"That's only natural, Lisa, that you'd like to be there, family's are suppose to pull together in times of a crisis," Tracy said, trying to comfort her daughter as Lanette opened the front door saying, "Grandma, your phone's ringing, you want me to answer it?"

"Lord yes! Now child, hurry before they think we're not home." Then taking Lisa Marie by the hand she said, "C'mon that might be Joe." Both of them walking toward the door, Lisa letting out a slight sigh and saying, "That would be a good thing mother."

Once inside they could see that Lanette was smiling and just talking away.

Lisa, letting out a giggle of relief, said, "It must be Joseph."

"It is Mom. It's Dad here. Go ahead. He wants to talk to you."

"I'll bet he better!" Lisa said, reaching for the phone. "Joseph, what's going on over there?"

"Well, they called alright and they want me to pick a track where I haven't been yet, someplace that the trainers will ride me on their horses."

"Where in the world is that going to be?" Lisa asked.

"We don't know, Lisa. Dad and I have been racking our brains trying to figure it out. We first thought about the track in Bossier

City, but hell, I don't know anyone there who wouldn't know my reputation. So many of those trainers come down from Hot Springs."

Lisa listened to her husband intently and then said, "Joe, what about any of the tracks in Texas?"

"That's an idea. What's Brian doing these days. Has he got any riders someplace?"

"Mom talked to him today. He was in Bossier, but I think he's planning on taking some apprentice to San Antonio."

"Lisa, ask your mom for his number. I need to talk with him about taking my book."

"Joe, I don't know about that, do you think it's a good idea?"

"Lisa, I want know that until I talk with him, but for now, I really don't have a choice."

"Well, hang on a minute and I'll ask her," Lisa said as she turned to her mother. "Mom, do you think Brain would help Joe out."

"That's something you'll have to talk with him about, I can't make any decisions for him, but here's his number. Better yet I'll call him myself and then if he want's to he can call Joe at his dad's."

"Joe, Mom's going to call him and see if he's willing to help. I guess he's still a little mad about you not letting him handle your book, back years ago."

"Damn, Lisa, that was so long ago, and besides I actually did him a favor. Look what happened to my career."

"Joe, are you sure me and the kids can't come over to Carrencro? I miss you so much."

"I miss you, too, baby, and the kids. Let's wait and see what Brian has to say, and then we'll decide what to do. But I promise we won't be apart much longer, just hang in there, okay?"

"Okay sweetheart. Look Joe, as soon as Brian calls you, let me know something please."

"I will, now let's get off the line so your mom can make the call, I love you, and tell the kids the same. I'll call back in a little while even if Brian doesn't call me."

"I love you, too, Joseph," Lisa Marie said, and then hung the phone up. Looking at her mother, she said, "Make the call, Mom, please."

"Oh, alright. Give me the telephone and then can I have a little privacy so I can talk this over with my husband?"

"Of course you can, Mom, I'll take the kids outside for a walk, how will that be?"

"It'll do y'all some good, the neighborhoods safe so enjoy the fresh air," Tracy said as she punched a number in that she knew by heart. While doing this she lit another cigarette.

"Bradly, Lanette, let's go for a walk, I need to talk with y'all," Lisa Marie told her children, sticking her head into the den, where they had been watching television.

Special Agent Conner, sitting hunkered down in his Trans Am just down the street from Tracy's house watched as Lisa Marie and her two children came outside, it was just about to turn dusk out, which Conner was glad for, the Louisiana sun could damn near torture a man, but it was cooling down a little bit now.

As the three Leblanc's strolled down the sidewalk, he wondered what they could be doing. What he wished though was that he wasn't going to have to wait until in the morning to get a phone tap.

It was a good thing that they weren't coming his way, however he would have liked to know what Lisa Leblanc was telling her kids, for the way her hands were swinging, she must have been saying a mouth full.

"Bradly, Lanette, I know that you kids think that the world must be coming to an end or at least that something very big is wrong."

Lisa Marie was trying to fill her children in on what was happening without doing more harm than good. But Joe and her had always tried to teach their children to be up front about things, however this whole thing had been kept from her. But she knew also that Joe had not felt he had a choice in the matter. Thinking about and choosing her next words carefully she continued. "The good news is, that the world's not coming to an end, at least not yet. But there are some bad people that have kidnaped your grandma Leblanc."

"Who's that?" Bradly asked.

"Even I know the answer to that one Brad!" Lanette offered.

"Well then tell me big shot Lanette."

"Now kids, this isn't the time for any of that," their mother said as she stopped walking and looked down into her son's eyes.

"Bradly, that's your dad's mother, and she's a real nice lady."

"Mama, why haven't I seen her before?" asked the youngster with uncertain eyes, looking back at his mother.

Lisa knew that behind those eyes, there were at least a hundred questions that she didn't want to answer out here on the sidewalk, "C'mon kids, let's head back to the house, Bradly, I'm going to answer all or at least try to answer your questions, and you too Lanette," Lisa said as they took the short walk back to her mother's yard.

"Now both of you sit down," Lisa said, pointing to some lawn chairs that her mother had. Taking a seat herself she took a deep breath and began. "Lanette, even before you were born all this got started, it's even looking like maybe it was starting when I was just a little girl. You see, my daddy, was a jockey, just like your father but he was killed a long time ago." Taking a minute and making sure that she kept her composure, she had to stay strong for her children, she couldn't let them see her breakdown. She then began again. "Well, for a while, we thought that he died because someone wanted to steal his money, but now we've found out that it may have been for other reasons."

"Why would they do that, Mom?" Lanette asked.

"So he'd be my grandpa?" Bradly said, having questions also that needed answers.

"That's right, Brad, he would be your Granddaddy Fontenot," Lisa returned.

"Fontenot?" Bradly repeated the name his mother had said, and then added, "Where did that name come from, Mom?"

Lanette, answering for her mother, said, "That was Mom's last name before she married Dad."

"That's right, Lanette, it sure was," Lisa Marie said, agreeing with her daughter. "Now let's go on with the story," she added, and as she did Tracy, came outside to join them saying, "There's no place like Louisiana in the evening, is there, Lisa Marie?"

"I'd have to agree with you on that, Mama." Lisa Marie then asked, "Did you talk with Brian?"

"I sure did, and with a little talking on my part, he said he'd be willing to help."

Lisa Marie didn't say it, although it was sure going through her mind. Wasn't that a crock, Brian, going to help us. He'd never in his life time had a jock with as much talent as Joe Leblanc. But then she also thought that she should be grateful. Now she also wondered what would the kidnappers want next, what was their long-term scheme, that's what she wanted to know. As she asked. "So, is he going to call Joe right away?"

"He said he would," her mother answered, and then asked, "Now what were y'all being so serious about when I came out here?"

"I was telling them about their Granddad Gerard."

"Oh, and just what were you telling them?" Tracy asked.

"Just that he had been a jockey like their dad was, and that he had been killed a long time ago. You know, Mother," Lisa continued.

"Lisa, I was proud of your father, but he's been gone a long time like you said, don't you think it's time to let it go?"

"Let it go! How can you say that?" Lisa Marie retorted, and then added, "Mom, I don't want to argue about this, believe me that's the last thing I want! So please don't be offended, but I'm going to finish this conversation with my children. If you don't want to listen then please give us some time to talk."

"Well! You don't have to be huffy about it, Lisa Marie."

"I'm not trying to be mother. I'm just trying to get through this."

"I realize that, but you have to know that it's hard for me also; however, I think I'll give y'all some time alone. Besides, I need to run down to the super market and get some breakfast food for the kids in the morning, how does that sound? This way, you can also talk to Joe, when he calls. I'll just get my pocketbook."

Tracy said as she walked through the door to her home.

Meanwhile, back in Carrencro, Joe had just gotten off of the phone with Brian Gunn.

"Dad, Brian said that he'd be willing to take my book in San Antonio and that he feels like he could get me on some good horses."

"Yeah, but does he know? I mean, did you explain what the deal was?" Charlie asked his son.

"You pretty much heard what I said. Although I have a feeling that Lisa's mother, filled in a lot of the blanks."

"I'll bet you're right, son. I'll tell ya, Joe, Tracy sure has changed a lot through the years. She and your mother used to be so close, but then she started going out with Brian when he moved down here. Hell, she even sold her part of the tack store and it was started, because of her, however, it's been a good investment for us. Your mom, just loves dealing with and seeing all the people that come in every day." Charlie's mind was drifting off as he said, "You know all the kids whose families work on the track, they come in there to get a soda or a candy bar and her eyes just light up. I know it's broken her heart not seeing you and our grandkids and Lisa, too, that girl, always was a favorite of your mother's."

"Dad, Lisa told me yesterday that she had talked with Mom, a few times through the years."

"Hell, Tee Joe, you think I didn't know! She didn't know I knew, though. Come on in here, I want to show you something." Charlie told his son as he got up from the kitchen table and motioning for Joseph to follow.

They went down the hall, with Joseph looking at the pictures on the wall. There were some win pictures of the elder Leblanc, winning some nice stake races for Joseph's grandfather Speck, there was a picture of Joe and Lisa's wedding, and various pictures through the years of Joe, and his mother and father, of Lisa, when she was pregnant with Lanette. But there was not one picture of Joe, winning any races, not even of the one where he won the Derby. Joe was thinking about that as he followed his father toward the room on the left at the end of the hall.

"Joseph, I know what you're thinking," Charlie said without turning around. "You're wondering why we took down the win pictures of you. Well, I made your mother do it. She didn't want to…"

Joe interrupted his father, by resting a hand on his shoulder and saying, "Dad, it's okay. Believe me, I understand."

The two had entered the bedroom that had been converted into a sewing room, crossing the floor to the walk in closet, Charlie opened the door. It was lined with coats and pants, old shirts and the like. "Looks pretty ordinary, wouldn't you think, son?" his father asked.

"Yeah, I guess so, Dad."

Parting back some of the shirts, Charlie said, "Look at that, Joe."

Joseph was amazed at what he saw but also it tugged at his heart something fierce. "I don't know what to say, Dad." For what he saw was not only the pictures that were missing from the wall in the hallway but also, pictures of him with his family, there was a small family portrait, and newspaper's, framed, hanging on the wall as well, ones that told the headline story of Joseph Leblanc, leading apprentice, there was even one telling about when he accepted the eclipse award, and winning the Derby. They were all there, all the big ones. The one other thing that stood out was that there were no negative new's clippings, nothing about questionable rides. Joseph, knew in his heart, at that moment that no matter what he'd done, his mother had not lost faith in her son. And somehow he knew also that his mother was being held somewhere against her will, but none the less, was her faith in Charlie and Joseph for she believed in her heart that they were coming for her. This thought burned in his soul that no matter what, he would not let her down!

Back in New Orleans, Agent Conner, was debating with himself in whether he should follow Tracy Gunn or stay and watch the daughter with her children, and so he called Russo.

"Russo here," he said.

"Yeah, it's me Conner. Look Mrs. Leblanc's mother is leaving. Should I stay with Mrs. Leblanc or follow the mom?"

"I'd say, stay with Leblanc, the mother's, just the mother, there should be no connection between her and the Headless Horseman."

"Alright, well, Russo, you know where I'm at then," Conner replied, and then disconnected wondering himself if the kidnapper's still had Maggie Leblanc, or was she already dead.

Russo himself was in a dark brown van about a quarter of a mile down from the Leblanc farm. And as he sat there in the back looking through a telescopic lens, he thought, there is no way this is going to be easy, matter of fact it was starting to look real complicated.

"Okay, Bradly, let's pick up where we left off, you too Lanette. Now where were we?" Lisa Marie asked, as her mother drove off down the street.

"Mom, you were telling me about Granddad," Bradly said, with anticipation in his voice.

"That's right, I was. Well, let's see. He was a good man, and I loved him very much. I didn't get to know him for very long, but I know he would have loved the both of you like there was no tomorrow." Lisa told her children these things as her mind slipped back in time to when she was about six years old. She could remember her dad and how he told her how special she was, and the way that he would play with her when he'd come home from work. And the times that she and her mother would go to the airport to pick her dad up after flying back from somewhere he had gone to ride a stake race, of course she hadn't known that at the time, only that he always brought her something back. Sometimes it would be one of those big lollipops that had swirls all thru them, or it might have been a teddy bear, or a book. Thinking back about those things almost brought a tear to her eyes.

"Are you alright, Mom?" Lanette asked, bringing her mother back from times way past.

"I'm fine." Lisa returned with a smile and then added, "Anyway, he's gone now, but you also have another granddad who is still living. That's who your dad's with now and I think you'll probably be meeting him before long. Of course, Lanette, you saw him a few times when you were just a little girl. You might remember him, but

I doubt it. Anyway, he's never seen you, Brad, although I believe that he may have seen pictures of both of y'all through the years."

"When are we going to see him?" Lanette asked.

"Soon, baby, very soon, I hope," Lisa Marie answered.

"What about the other grandma?" asked Bradly.

"Well, kids, some very bad people have her right now, and that's what your dad and granddad are doing right now. They're trying to get her back."

"Mom, did Dad break the law? And what about those men who were chasing him back in Rapid City?" Lanette asked her mother.

"Now both of you, listen real good. Yes, your father did some things that were against the law, but sometimes there are reasons that people do things that are beyond their control. That doesn't mean that it's alright, only that there are times that you will have to make decisions and when that time comes you hope you make the right one."

"So will Dad have to go to jail?" asked Brad.

"I honestly don't know, I just don't know. But no matter what, we're going to stand behind your father, one hundred percent. That's what families do," Lisa Marie told them with a certain pride in her voice.

Getting up from her chair she said, "c'mon kids, let's go call your father, I think we could all use a Joe Leblanc pep talk."

However, upon walking into the house the phone began ringing. Lisa Marie picking it up on the second ring said "Hello."

"It's me, Lisa, Joe, I talk…" He didn't get to finish as Lisa Marie cut in saying, "Oh Joseph, the kids and I were just going to call you."

"Well, looks like I beat you to it," he said with a little laugh.

"Seriously though Lisa, I just got off the phone with Brian, about fifteen minutes ago. He and I decided that he would represent me for mounts in San Antonio."

"Did you tell him what this is all about?" His wife asked.

"Not really, I was hoping that your mother clued him in a little."

"Oh, I'm sure she did. Anyway, he didn't say anything, about when he wanted to be your agent, and you wouldn't let him?"

"Not a word, now you know what I would like?"

"What's that Joseph?" Lisa asked skeptically.

"Well, there's two things, actually three but I can only tell you two of them, you'll have to use your imagination on the third. First, I want to talk with my children, next I want to see y'all."

Holding the phone out Lisa said, "Which ones first?" Brad was faster as he grabbed the telephone saying "Dad!"

"Bradly, that's not fair! Mom!" Declared Lanette.

"You'll get your turn," Lisa told her daughter with a smile as she motioned Lanette to come sit next to her. Which Lanette did. Lisa slid her arm around her saying "I love you sweetheart."

"I love you, too, Mom."

While all of these thing's transpired there was a thirty-six-foot motor home, parked behind a barn in Folsom, Louisiana. Folsom is a small town just across Lake Ponchatrain near New Orleans. It was mainly a bunch of smaller farms that had racehorse training tracks where some trainers sent their young horses to get them ready to go to the tracks to race.

"Why are you doing this to me?" Maggie Leblanc asked the man, adding, "I haven't done anything to you."

She had no idea where she was at, only that she sometimes caught the slight smell of horse manure. The last thing she could remember before waking up with her hands and feet bound was that she had receive a call f rom someone that had said, her husband Charlie, had been involved in an accident, but not to worry, he was fine. He just needed her to come to the Wal-Mart parking lot and pick him up. She had though nothing of it; why would she consider foul-play? There was no reason that she should. So she had gotten in her car and simply drove to the Wal-Mart. She had seen her husbands truck or so she had thought it was his truck. Now she wasn't so sure. It had been parked next to a motor home, she had gotten out of her car, and she had seen the dent in the truck, and commented on it to someone whom she thought was Charlie, who had his back to her, and was talking to someone inside the motor home, but then she came up behind him, she had said, "Charlie, baby, are you alright?" That's when this man turned around and it wasn't Charlie!" How could she have made that mistake? But then he grabbed her and put something over her mouth as he dragged her into the camper on wheels. That was the last thing she remembered until now.

"I've known you since you were just a kid! Why would you do this?"

"Shut up, old lady, or else I'm puttin' you back to sleep," the man said.

Outside, a horn blew, the man looked at Maggie, with eyes full of contempt and said, "Say one word," and showing her some kind of pistol, added. "It makes no difference to me, dead or alive." He then got up to step outside, leaving Maggie to contemplate her situation. She was smart enough not to try and yell out for help, and there was no way she could get loose from the way she was connected to the chain running from the floor. She was wondering though who belonged to the horn that had blown outside. She was also thinking about her husband Charlie, "God," she said softly, "please, let Charlie, be alright." And silently Maggie Leblanc said a prayer for her husband, her family, and finally for herself.

Across the lake in New Orleans, Lanette Leblanc, had just finished talking with her dad.

"Okay, honey, it's me," Lisa Marie said, and then told the children to go into the den and watch TV so that Joe and her could talk.

"Joseph, what are we going to do?" Lisa asked her husband.

"All we can do is wait until tomorrow to see what the Headless Horseman, want's us to do. But I was thinking that I'd like for y'all to come on over here. This is not a time for us to be apart. I think it would be safe at least as safe as anywhere," he told his wife as she listened.

"Oh, that sounds so good, Joseph," she exclaimed. "When can we come?" she asked.

"Well, I don't know when the kidnappers will call but if y'all left in the morning early enough, it'd be good if y'all were here by noon, what do you think?"

"Joe, that sounds great, but what if Mom doesn't want to come?"

"Y'all must not be gett'n along that well."

"It's not really that Joseph, I think that all this talk about Dad, has brought up some memories that she doesn't want to deal with."

"Lisa, I can't really say as I blame her. But didn't she want to come over here from the beginning to check on Dad? And besides that don't you think she'll want to be with y'all while she can?"

"Baby, all I can do is ask her," Lisa said, then added, "but it'll have to wait until she get's back from the grocery store."

"Well, how about I call you early in the morning, say six thirty or so."

"That sounds good to me sweetheart, me and the kids are exhausted. As a matter of fact, as soon as we get off the phone, I'm putting the children to bed, they've had a hard two days."

"Lisa Marie, I'm sorry for all I've put y'all through…"

"Joseph, stop it, I know you had your back against the wall, so don't apologize for something you couldn't control," she told her husband and then, choosing her next words carefully, she continued, "Joe, I've never asked you to quit the drugs because I figured you had your reasons and even if you weren't making six digits, you still provided for us. But, honey, please, since we're cleaning all this up will you try to quit for me and the children?"

"Lisa, I've put y'all through a lot, but I promise, I'll do my very best to clean my life up."

"Joseph, that's all I can expect, that you'll try."

"Things are going to be a lot different, I promise. Now I hate to, however we need to get some rest, so tell the kids again that I love them and I love you too, baby, more than words can say."

"I love you too, Joe, and so do the kids, but you know that by now, I'm sure, so I'll talk to you in the morning."

Lisa Marie was sitting on the couch thinking about the conversation she'd had with her husband, for only a few minutes when she heard her mother pull up.

She quickly went out to help her mother with whatever groceries she had bought, which turned out to be very little. Actually only some milk, eggs, and some bacon.

"Mom, where'd you go to? I was starting to worry just a little."

"Oh, I went by old Mrs. Pujols, to see if she needed anything from the store. Her husband passed on about six months ago and I've kind of started a habit of checking on her at least once a day."

Tracy told her daughter as the two walked back into the house.

"That's good, Mom, it gives you something to do," Lisa Marie said as she placed the milk and thing's in the fridge. "Mom, I talked with Joe and, as you already know I'm sure, Brian's going to be his agent over in San Antonio."

Cutting in, Tracy said, "I'm glad that Brian can help, and really I'm surprised that he is. You know it hurt him pretty bad when Joe wouldn't hire him for an agent."

"Mom, even I know that it wouldn't have worked, Brian didn't know anybody in New York. You gotta have clientele, in order to do a jock any good, especially when you've reached the caliber that Joe had." Lisa Marie was trying to explain without getting upset. "And besides, mother, what was Joe to do, fire the agent he had. Hell, old Harry, had handled Joe, for three years, the two had made each other."

"Well, old Harry, couldn't even keep Joe at the top, now could he?"

"That's not fair and you know it," Lisa said, and then asked, "Where do you want the kids to sleep, it's been a long day and we all just need some rest. Can we finish talking about this in the morning?" Lisa Marie had already decided that she would rent a car to drive her and the children to Carrencro. She knew now why she had stayed away for so long. Why couldn't her mother just accept that Brian, however good of a guy he was just wasn't the type of agent, Joe liked working with. If not for this situation, they wouldn't be working together now.

"Yes, Lisa, I suppose you're right, let's put the kids in my bed, you can have the bed in the spare room, and I'll bed down there in the den. I fall asleep in there half the time anyway watching television."

Later that night with the kids asleep, her mother in the den, Lisa Marie Leblanc, lay in bed thinking of Maggie, her mother in law.

Maggie had been such a special person in Lisa's life, even early on. Lisa prayed that she would be alright. And as she thought about her, she slipped from the covers and knelt beside the bed and said a silent prayer for Joseph's mother.

In Carrencro, Joe and Charlie had just called it a day themselves. Joseph had been dead on his feet when he finally closed his eyes while in his dad's old recliner, Charlie himself had dozed off on the couch while Joe was still talking to Lisa Marie. Joe had gotten up, found a blanket and covered his father as he slept. Thinking, I sure do love you, Dad.

Down the road from the small farm while Joe and his father slept, Agent Russo was he himself beginning to feel the results of lots of miles and little sleep. The van that he was in was more than likely going to draw suspicion if he didn't move it come morning. The wire tap had produced very little information other than, all those concerned were now in a waiting game.

Russo after listening to the last phone call made to the Leblanc's, before Joe had called his wife, a call came in from someone named Brian Gunn. Not knowing at first who he was, Russo running the usual checks quickly learned that he indeed was a self-proclaimed jockey agent that usually hustled no name riders. The one thing that surprised him more than anything was the fact that he was married to Lisa Leblanc's mother. Russo also knew that this game of cat and mouse was once again going to be on the move. But this time the F.B.I. had the jump, for they knew where the next game would be played, giving the agents time to stack the deck just a little. And in any kind of fight the first punch means a lot. Russo laying his head down on the make shift bed in the van thought, "Just a short nap want hurt…" His eyes closed before the thought was finished.

Lisa Marie opened her eyes as her nose took in the sweet smell of bacon frying in the kitchen, letting her know that her mother was already at work putting breakfast together.

Laying there Lisa began thinking about her mother, and their relationship, she wished that things had been different with them. But, then her mother should have never got in the middle of Joe's business by pushing Brian on him. Joe had been very adamant about not letting Brian be his agent.

Brian and her mother had been through a rough couple of years as far as money was concerned. And then somehow he had talked Tracy into selling the house in Carrencro, and not long after that she had sold her half of the tack shop to Maggie. Then Brian and her had moved to New Orleans. That's about the time that Tracy had called Lisa, asking to borrow money, which Joe at the time had been the leading rider in the nation, money was flowing. Joe had no problem with sending money. At times the sums were pretty hefty. But her mother was always saying that Brian's riders would soon be winning races, and then they would be able to pay the money back. Of course it never happened. Brian's jockey's did win some races along the way, at places like St. Louis, Kansas and New Orleans in the winter. But she still said, they needed money for one reason or another. Finally Joe had called the loans, enough is enough he had said. He knew just about what Brian was making by keeping up with the races that his jockey's won.

Tracy had said they couldn't pay, and then she had made the comment to Lisa that to keep the money that Joseph was making in the family, he should fire his agent and hire Brian. Well needless to say, Joe had flipped. He couldn't believe that they could even suggest such a thing. That's when the whole thing had come to a sudden halt. Tracy stopped calling and Joe quit sending money and before you knew it they weren't talking at all, or if they did, it was very seldom. What was weird though, was the fact, that in less than two years, Joe's career had dammed near bottomed out.

Through the years the tension between Lisa and her mother had slowly diminished, or so it had seemed.

Lisa just wished that thing's as a whole, were different between them. These thoughts were roaming her mind as the telephone rang. Lisa, turning to the night stand to see the time, said, "damn, is it six thirty already?" But seeing that it was about five minutes till six added, "Must not be Joe, but she listened anyway to see if her mother called her name. She didn't.

Lisa Marie, yawning, got out of bed and throwing the housecoat around her that her mother had loaned her padded down the hallway and as she went into the bathroom she heard her mother say.

"Brian, baby, when will you be home?" But that's all Lisa heard as she closed the door, and climbed into the shower. Fifteen minutes later she emerged from the bathroom, housecoat clad, towel rapped around her head and feeling like an almost new person.

"Good morning, sunshine," Tracy greeted her daughter.

"Mom, you haven't called me sunshine, since I was a teenager. But good morning to you as well, have you heard anything out of the kids, this morning?" Lisa Marie asked.

"Not a peep, bless their hearts. They must have been all done in, would you like some coffee?"

"That would be great, is it Community coffee?"

"Lisa Marie, have you ever known me to drink any other kind?"

"No, I don't guess I have," she answered, then stated, "You seem to be in a good mood this morning."

"I'll tell ya, Lisa, I thought a lot about what you said yesterday and well, I think it's time that we try to get along. If you believe that Joseph's telling the truth about all of this, well then, I'm behind y'all completely. I just don't want to dig up memories. So I'm going to stay out of the way. I pray that Maggies safe, and I hope that Brian, can be some help to Joe. As a matter of fact, I just got off of the phone with Brian."

"Whats he doing Mom?"

"Well, he's on his way, should be here around two-o-clock, maybe stay the night then head over to Carrencro, to meet with Joe."

"Has he talked with Joseph this morning?" Lisa asked

"He didn't say whether he had or not, I just assumed that he had," Tracy answered as she filled two coffee cups handing one to her daughter.

"Mom, Joe wants me and the kids to come over to Carrencro today…"

"Well, here's an idea, if you want you can take my car on over then I can ride with Brian when he goes to meet Joe."

"Are you sure, Mom, you wouldn't mind if I did that?"

"Not at all Lisa, that way y'all could spend some time together before the men head to Texas."

That didn't sound right, because Lisa Marie had every intention of going with her husband to San Antonio. But she wasn't going to say anything that might upset the apple cart. Tracy seemed to be a lot less uptight about this whole situation, and Lisa Marie sure as hell wanted to keep it that way.

"Joseph's going to call in a few minutes, Mom. I'm going to wake the kids, then I'll help you finish breakfast.

If it's alright with you, I'd just as soon get on the road, as quick as we can get ready," Lisa said as she started for her mother's room where the children were still asleep.

"Of course I don't mind, I know y'all are anxious to see Joe," Tracy said, and then asked, "How many eggs can the kids eat?"

"Oh, Mom, just scramble about a half dozen, with the bacon and toast, that should be plenty for all of us," Lisa said as she unwrapped the towel from her hair and hanging it on the door knob of the bathroom. She then knocked on the door of her mother's room saying, "C'mon, kids, rise and shine!" Then ducking into the spare room to pull on a pair of jeans and tee shirt from the Sturgis Bike Rally, she knocked on the door again and opening it said, "Get up, lazy head, we're going to see your father. Hey, Lanette, Bradly, quit playing games! It's to early." But even as she said that, something very chilling started claiming her body and before she could say another word, she knew in her heart, that something very bad had happened while she had slept the night away. And as this fear, over took her, the telephone began to ring. Turning to run down the hall, she cried, "Mom, I've got it, don't answer it, I got it!"

"What in the world is wrong with you Lisa Marie?" Her mother asked, sounding very alarmed.

"The kids, mother, my children, they're gone!"

The telephone kept ringing and everything seemed in slow motion, like she couldn't move fast enough, reaching the phone she snatched it up, thinking it to be her husband. She answered saying, "Joseph!" But it wasn't Joseph, for the most horrifying voice, she had ever heard said, "Try, try as she might, poor lil Joe's wife's children, have gone out of sight. The Headless Horseman rides again, ah, but he'll be in touch!" And then the phone went dead with Lisa Marie unable to stand, dropped to her knee's and softly cried.

"Lisa Marie, what in the world is wrong with you?" Tracy asked, as she knelt by her daughter. "Who was that?"

"Mama," Lisa said, "They took my kids, how could they get to them? Didn't you have the doors locked?"

"Of course, I had the doors locked,Lisa, this is New Orleans!" her mother said, "You have to call the police, Lisa, let me get the number for you, or better yet just dial 911."

"I'm not calling the police," saying that, she pulled a card from her back pocket. "I'm calling somebody else." Then she started pressing buttons.

"Who, who are you calling? You should be calling the police," Tracy said as she went to turn the stove off.

When she walked back into the living room, her daughter was talking with someone on the phone. "Yes, I understand, Mr. Russo, I'll be right here waiting." And then she replaced the phone in it's cradle only to pick it up again.

"Now who are you calling?" Tracy asked her daughter, without saying anything, Lisa was again punching numbers.

"Lisa Marie, I asked you, who you were calling!"

"I'm calling my husband, mother, is that okay?" Without waiting for her mother to answer she entered the last three digits and then waited.

"Hello." It was Charlie who picked up.

"Charlie, it's me Lisa," she said, having a difficult time keeping her emotions in check.

Charlie automatically sensed something wrong, "Lisa, what's the matter?"

"It's the kids, Charlie, they took the kids!"

"Who took them?"

"Somebody called and said it was the Headless Horseman, where is Joseph?"

"He's right here," Charlie said, handing his son the phone.

"Lisa, what's wrong? What's this about the children!" Joseph Leblanc asked his wife.

"The crazy bastard, that took your mother, somehow got in this house and took our children."

There was silence on both ends of the line until Lisa Marie, began to speak again. "Well, Joseph, what have you got to say?"

"I don't know what to say Lisa, I just don't know," Joseph told his wife.

"Well, I called Russo, evidently there has been some agent, watching this house since we arrived yesterday, he's suppose to be calling him now to see what he saw, if anything. I just don't believe this is happening," Lisa said, almost in tears again.

The door bell rang once then twice. "Mom, that's probably the agent, from the F.B.I."

"I'll get it, you just keep Joe on the line," Tracy said to Lisa Marie.

Thirty seconds later, three agents came into the living room, one of them saying, "Mrs. Leblanc, we need to talk with you."

"Joe, I think I better call you back, I love you," she said and then laid the phone down. These guys didn't look happy, like they might have some bad news. Standing up she asked, "Which one of y'all was watching this house last night? How in the hell could you have let some maniac, come into this home and take two kids out and not done something about it." Lisa Marie's anger was starting to rise taking the place of despair and fear. Before they could respond, she started in on them again. "I mean aren't y'all federal agents, trained in this sort of thing?"

"Mrs. Leblanc, please let me explain," one of them said.

"Well, someone damn sure better start explaining something!" She demanded.

The same agent answered, "Ma'am, my name is David Pearce, and as you probably know we're with the F.B.I. And, yes ma'am, there was an agent, that had you under surveillance, however, Agent Conner was found stabbed to death in his car just a few minutes ago."

"Oh, sweet Jesus, I am so sorry, Mr. Pearce," Lisa Marie said.

"Mrs. Leblanc, we can't let this information out, for fear that it would effect the outcome of this investigation. We have forensic people on their way to go over the abduction site."

Lisa Marie felt the word abduction site, hit her like a ton of bricks. It somehow didn't seem real, like maybe this was one big bad nightmare and soon it would be morning and she would wake up and everything would really be normal. But she knew in her heart that even though it seemed like a nightmare it was for real and the stakes just kept getting higher and higher.

Meanwhile, over in Carrencro, Joe Leblanc and his father Charlie, were at the kitchen table. "Dad, what am I gonna do? They got my children," Joseph said, putting his head down on the table.

Charlie rested his hand on Joe's shoulder and began. "Son, I know that it seems like they got us over a barrel, and maybe they do. So we gotta play their game for a minute or two, but we'll get our turn, we're gonna get Lisa Marie over here, we're gonna watch each others backs and we're gonna catch these bastards with their pants down," Charlie Leblanc said with the constitution of a mule.

"Dad," Joseph said.

"Yeah."

"Do you think Mom and the kids are going to be alright?"

"Joseph, I just don't know, they're in Gods hands, right now and all we can do, is to do exactly what these people want us to do." Charlie was trying to be optimistic with his son, when the phone rang. Both men reached for it. "Go ahead, son," Charlie said.

Joe picked it up on the third ring. "Hello," he said nervously.

"Joseph, are you mad?" Said the voice of the Headless Horseman.

"What have you done with my children?" Joe asked, without answering the man's question.

"You didn't answer my question, Joseph."

"I'm pissed, is that what you want to hear? You hurt my children freak and I'll hunt you down! Are we on the same page?"

"I don't answer questions, I ask them. Now answer this, what track did you pick?"

"San Antonio."

"Good, do you have an agent?"

"Yes, Brian Gunn".

"Um, that figures, well Joe, I gotta go, I've got something to set up for you, I'll call back at twelve noon, by the way, Lanette and Bradly are enjoying their grandmothers company. Click." The call was ended.

"What did he say, Joe?" Charlie asked.

"Said he'd call back at noon, and that the kids were with Mom, he didn't think much of my choice of agents, though, I can tell you that."

"I'm not real high on Brian myself, Joseph, but he's what we have to work with."

"Yeah, I know what you mean, Dad, although on the other hand he knows a lot more people over there than I do."

"How long do you think we're going to have to stay there?" Charlie asked his son.

"Dad, I have no idea, do you think old Rusty's gonna take good care of your horses over at the track?"

"Oh, of course he will, there's no worries there, I can promise you that, Rusty's as dependable as the rain," Charlie said of his friend.

"I guess I better call Lisa Marie."

"You tell her to high tail it over here. We need to be all in one spot. That's where our mistake was. We were spread out too much," Charlie said as the phone rang again. This time Charlie answered it. "Hello, Charlie Leblanc here," he said.

"Mr. Leblanc, this is Agent Russo. Look, I've got three agents, with your daughter-in-law right now. I need you to meet me at the Oppalousas airfield in one hour and bring your son with you."

"What for? What have you got up your sleeve now, Russo?" Charlie asked.

"I can't explain and I've got to go, you just be there!" Click.

"Damn-it all to hell, here I am, seventy something years old and all of a sudden, every Tom, Dick and Harry want's to start order'n me around!" Charlie said as he hung up the phone.

"Who was that, Dad?" asked Joseph.

"That damned Russo, from the F.B.I. He wants us to meet him at the airstrip, over in Oppalousas, in an hour."

"What for? Did he say?"

"No, just that he had three agents with Lisa Marie right now."

"I better call her," he said as he picked up the phone and punched in his mother in laws number in New Orleans.

"Hello," Tracy said as she picked up the telephone.

"Tracy, it's me Joe. Let me speak to Lisa, please!"

"She's not here, Joseph, the F.B.I. took her someplace," Tracy answered.

"How long has she been gone?"

"About twenty minutes, Joe, it looks like the people, that took the kids, killed an agent last night. Have you heard anything from them?"

"About ten minutes ago, the kidnappers called, saying that the kids were with Mom, they didn't say what kind of shape they were in. We can only pray. Tracy, Dad and I have to be someplace but we want be gone long. I think I know where they took Lisa, and if I'm right, she'll be here the next time we talk."

"Joseph, you have her call me if you see her, okay?"

"I will. Now, I've got to go." Listening to her say goodbye, he set the telephone down, saying to his father. "Dad, I'm pretty sure that we'll be seeing Lisa Marie before long."

"You think they're flying her over here?" Charlie asked.

"I believe so, Dad. Let's go see," Joseph said, getting up from the table. Charlie Leblanc, putting on his cowboy hat said, "Tee Joe, I'm gett'n way to old, for this kind of stuff, way to old."

"Me too, Dad, me too!" Joseph returned, as the two walked out of the house to Charlie's pickup truck.

Little did they know that not only was the F.B.I. watching them, there was yet another member of the Headless Horseman group, that had their eyes trained on the father and son duo.

Twenty minutes later, Joe and Charlie were sitting at the airstrip, outside of Oppalousas, when they saw a brown colored van pull into the tiny airport, if you could call it that. The van pulled up beside them, with Agent Russo, stepping from the vehicle saying, "Well, I see you made it."

The two Leblanc's also got out of their truck with Joseph saying, "Looks like me and you get around, Russo."

"Yeah, Joseph, I guess you're right about that. When we started this thing, I never dreamed that it would elevate to this."

"Well, it sure as hell, has gotten out of hand, but you know what?"

"What's that?"

"If you would have just let me alone, I'd have stiffed that horse in Rapid City, sure some people would have made some money and some would have lost, but my mother, would be home with my dad, and my children, wouldn't be with some maniac, right now."

"I'll have to admit we have made some big mistakes," Russo replied.

"Mistakes! Is that what you call 'em; mistakes! I arta knock you on your cou'yon ass!"

"My what?'

"It's Cajun, for stupid," Charlie said, trying not to laugh.

"Whoop-whoop-whoop," the three turned toward the approaching helicopter, with Russo telling them, "Lisa Marie's on that chopper, courtesy of the F.B.I."

"I kind of figured that; Agent Russo, and for that, I thank you," said Joe while he and the other two covered their eyes keeping the dirt out of them that was being kicked up from the landing helicopter.

Meanwhile, there was a reunion of sorts going on over in Folsom, Louisiana.

"Are you my grandma?" Bradly asked the woman lying on the bed beside him and his sister.

"Well, I might be. Are you Bradly?" she asked.

"Yeah, I'm Bradly Leblanc, and this is my sister, Lanette."

"Yes, I'm your grandmother, and I knew who you were, why you look just like your daddy did when he was about your age, and Lanette, you're the spittin' image of your mother."

"I am?" Lanette asked and then before Maggie could answer that question, Bradly, fired another one her way. "Why do they have us here?"

"Bradly, I have no idea?"

"Grandma," Lanette said, "This has something to do with Daddy, and horse racing, he's with his dad, right now."

"Are you sure, Lanette, about that?"

"I'm positive," Lanette answered

"Well, I guess you better start at the beginning because none of this makes any sense."

"I think it has something to do with our mama's daddy, about when he got killed."

"Gerard?" Maggie said, sounding very confused, and then gave full attention to what Lanette had to say.

In Oppalousas, after being reunited with her husband and father in law, the three had driven back to the Leblanc farm, in Carrencro. Lisa had been full of questions at least till she broke down crying with Joe trying to comfort her. "Baby we're going to get them back, I promise."

Charlie himself was doing some thinking on his own. Actually it was about a movie he'd seen once, he couldn't remember which one, not that it was important, although it's contents were. It had a kidnaping plot to it, a ransom had been made, and an exchange had been planned, however since the victim had seen her assailants face they couldn't let her go, it was never in the plan anyway.

Charlie in his heart knew that unless they could find out who had taken his wife and now his grandchildren and where they had been taken, well, he doubted very seriously that they would be released, no matter what Joe was going to do in Texas. He silently said a prayer as he was brought back from his thoughts.

"Dad, it's almost time for them to call," Joseph told his father.

Cutting in, Lisa Marie said, "Joe, do you think that they might let us talk to the kids?"

"I don't know, most of the time they do all of the talkin' and if I do cut in and say anything hell, they hang up."

In the brief silence of the three as they contemplated their thoughts the phone began to ring. "You answer Tee Joe," his father said.

Picking it up, Joseph said, "Hello."

"Well, well, I see that Jack and Diane are together again, how is the lovely Lisa Marie? Ah, don't answer, there's no need, you see I took a glimpse at her last night." Laughter rang in Joseph's ear as the man continued. "But seriously, Joe, the race is about to start. When's your new agent going to be there?"

Answering he said, "In the morning."

"Wrong answer, you and him will be at the track in San Antonio tomorrow."

"But..." Joe started, it was to late though, the caller had disconnected the line.

"Damn it! Damn it all to hell!" Joseph said as he slammed the telephone down.

"What did he say?" Lisa asked

"We have to get in touch with Brian, they want us in San Antonio, in the morning."

"We'll do what he said, call Brian and tell him to get his ass on the move." Lisa Marie told her husband. And then picked the phone up herself to call her mother to see if Brian had gotten there yet.

Over in Folsom, Maggie was telling her grandchildren. "Jesus, it seems like all hell's broken loose."

"I don't like this," Bradly said.

At that moment the door to the motor home opened.

"Well now, are y'all gettin' acquainted?" the man who had entered asked, laughing.

"Why are we here? Why are you doing this?" Maggie asked.

"Be quite, don't start asking me a lot of questions that I can't or won't answer. We'll be traveling tonight and don't go ask'n where to because I ain't sayin'," the man told them.

"I just don't understand what you want with us," Maggie said, and then added. "You always were into something though, but this just makes no sense at all. What could you gain from this."

"I'll tell ya what I'm gain'n, I've watched Joe Leblanc's career go right down the tube, and now he's going to make us a lot of money and then I can watch him suffer."

"What did my daddy ever do to you, that you'd hate him so much?" Lanette asked.

"What did he do," I'll tell you what he did, he always though he was so this and so that. But look at him now."

"That doesn't tell me what he did," said Lanette.

"He didn't do anything but be a good boy, everybody liked your father, and then he became a great jockey. Everyone all around southern Louisiana, was proud of Joe," Maggie told her grandchildren.

"Shut up old woman, before I…"

"Before you what? Beat me up!!!… that'd be about right, you beat'n up on an old woman!"

"You better leave her alone!" Bradly piped up.

"Aw, the hell with y'all," the man said as he opened the door and stepped out.

""He's not going to let us go, is he?" asked Lanette.

Not wanting to worry her grandchildren, Maggie said, "Of course he is." But she wasn't so sure, the reason being they or at least she knew exactly who he was. Had known him most of his life. Although she doubted very seriously that he had thought this up on his own, he just wasn't that smart. And then she thought about what Lanette had said, about this being connected someway to Gerard Fontenot's, death. There was no way that he could be connected to something that had happened so long ago, he just wasn't that old. Somewhere, she was missing something, she just didn't know what.

"What did she say Lisa," Joe asked, after his wife got off of the phone.

"She said, that he was on his way and that she would call him on his cell phone, to make sure that he came straight there."

"I wonder what time he'll get there?" Charlie asked.

"I don't know, but it's only one o'clock, if he was on his way he should be here no later than about three at the very least," Joe answered.

"Joseph, what about riding tack, all your stuffs back in Rapid City?" His wife asked.

Charlie kinda chuckled a little as he said, "That's not gonna be a problem considering his mother owns a tack shop. Why don't we go on over and get what you need."

"Sounds like a winner, Dad. Lisa, call your mom, and ask her to call Brian and have him meet us at mom's tack shop."

Agent Russo had changed vehicles and was now in a PT Cruiser, sitting in the parking lot of Cajun Downs. He had been listening to the bug he had hidden in the Leblanc's kitchen and now he was just waiting for them to pass. It was always good, if you could stay a jump ahead. "And there they go," he said, to himself as they pulled through the gate. Russo was anxious to see this Brian guy. He'd run checks on him up and down the pike and had came up dry. The guy was clean as far as he could see. But at this point everybody was a suspect, which he was now running through his mind, the players that had anted up. There was Joseph, the jockey, who was known for not letting some of his mounts run. Did he actually know who the Headless Horseman was, and the kidnaping of his mother, just a ploy to get the heat off himself. And then we have the lovely Lisa Marie, the ever loving wife, that has stood behind her husband as Hillary had with the President. Maybe though she was the driving force just as Hillary had been to Old Bill. Let's take a little closer look at Lisa Leblanc. She seemed real nice, but let's look at fact number one, the day that Maggie had been kidnaped. Lisa said, she had been approached by a man with a dark suit and dark sunglasses, she had assumed that he was an F.B.I. agent, telling her to wait at the far end of the grandstand. A quick scan of the gambling structure produced no one of the description that Lisa Marie had given. And her husband, had fled that day. Was the dark suit, fictional, just an illusion so that Joe could get away. What about when the kids, had been kidnaped, were they really or had Lisa Marie taken them someplace? But then he would have to look at her as a killer for someone had offed Agent Conner. He doubted very seriously, if Lisa was in on it, however, he wasn't going to let a great smile and a sweet ass, blur his vision. Next would be…let's see now, he thought. Charlie Leblanc, Joe's dad. Without another thought, he scratched the old Cajun, from the suspect pile though, along with his wife. And then before he could search his brain any further, a Chrysler, pulled through the gate coming to a stop in front of the Tack Shop owned by the elder Leblancs.

A man of about…say late fifty's, stepped from the car and walked up to the door. Russo didn't have a lot to go on but he figured that this must be Brian Gunn, he just looked like an ex-jockey, short, kinda cockey in his walk. Still didn't look like he had put on much weight from his riding days.

As he knocked on the door, it was opened by Lisa Marie. Brian or at least he though it to be Brian stepped through the doorway, leaving Russo to his thoughts after jotting down the plate number on the Chrysler.

He picked up his cell phone from the seat, punched in a number, pressed send, then waited…ring…ring…r "Hello."

"Yeah, this is Russo, how did the forensic people make out?" he asked the voice on the other end.

"Just a second, I've got the report right her…okay, here it is. Looks like on the carpet they found traces of horse manure, sediment that may have come from the bayou or lake, there were no prints except for the occupants of the home, and no forced entry."

"That's it?" Russo asked.

"Yes, sir, that's all I have at this time."

"Call me with anything else you guys come up with," Russo said. And then ended the call just about the time that four people came walking out. Three, he knew for sure, one of them he could only speculate.

Joe was carrying what looked like a oversized gym bag, full of something. If Russo had to guess, he'd say that it carried the things you have to have in order to ride races. The Leblanc's got into Charlie's pickup and the newcomer in his own vehicle. Then they promptly left the grounds heading in the direction of the Leblanc farm. Thirty minutes after they arrived they were once again pulling out on to the highway. This time, Charlie also was carrying a bag of what may have been clothes. Lisa Marie and Joe had decided to take his fathers pick-up so that they could talk, while Charlie and Brian would ride together.

Agent Russo was tucked in behind them at a safe distance as not to be spotted. The Leblanc's knew he was there, Brian did not.

They had pulled onto Interstate ten, headed west.

"Joseph, who do you think is behind this?" Lisa Marie asked her husband as she settled in for the long ride to San Antonio.

"Baby, I've been racking my brain trying to figure it out but I just don't know."

"And this has been going on since when?" Lisa Marie asked.

"For twelve long years, I've sure made somebody a lot of money Lisa. I do know this though, it's got to be somebody that knows us really well. And every now and then I catch the hint of a Cajun accent, but he's trying to cover it up, know what I mean?"

"Yeah, I do, but who could have been around since my father was killed?" Lisa Marie asked.

"I have no idea, Lisa, I just don't know."

The car following was Charlie and Brian, the two were trying to feel each other out a little. "So what've you been doing with yourself these day's Brian?" Charlie asked, as he from time to time glanced out of the passengers window.

"Not to much Charlie, been hustle'n a couple of riders up in Bossier, that's about it."

"Well, what do you make of what's going on with this Headless Horseman guy."

"Charlie, hell I don't know. Tracy filled me in on a little of it but she didn't know a lot herself. What I find hard to believe, is that somebody killed an F.B.I. agent, less than a hundred yards from our house."

"Hell, the killer was in your house," Charlie said.

"Yeah, I know, I just pray that the kids, and your wife, are alright Charlie. As far as speculation to who it may be, me, I ain't gotta clue." This, Brian told Charlie as they rolled down I-ten.

In Folsom, an R.V. was pulling on to the highway. In the back were three people tied to a chain that was bolted to the floor. They were scared because they didn't know what the future held for them The door was closed to the room that was at the back of the motor home, at one time, there had been windows but now they were sealed off to where you couldn't see out, or see in.

"Where are they taking us, grandma?" Bradly asked.

"Child, I have no idea, but Bradly, we're going to be alright, I promise." Maggie tried being optimistic, but in her heart she herself was also scared, first for her grandchildren and then for herself. One thing she knew helped to ease her fear was the fact that in all the years that she had known Charlie Leblanc, he had never let her down, not one time.

"Grandma?" said Lanette.

"Yes, darlin'," answered Maggie.

"Are these people going to hurt my mom and dad?"

"I don't think so…but come on now, let's close our eyes and try and get some sleep, you never know when the good lord's going to open a door and we have to be ready to run!" The two children did close their eyes and drifted off to sleep, they were exhausted from all they had been through. Ms. Maggie, however, lay there with her eyes open thinking, where are you taking us you little bastard?

After arriving in San Antonio, the Leblanc's had rented two rooms at the extended Stay Inn, Brian and Charlie would stay in one, and Lisa and Joseph would stay in the other.

Russo, had also checked into the same motel.

They were now in the racing office at Texas Downs.

Brian and Joseph were registering as agent and jockey. Joseph was told that he would have to see the stewards before he would be allowed to ride at the Texas oval. After reviewing his past, the State Steward, asked. "Joseph, why have you come to our track to ride?"

"Because I'm trying to turn my life around, I'm just trying to establish new ground," Joseph told the three stewards that governed the track.

After deliberating among themselves for just a few minutes, they returned their attention to Joe. "Mr. Leblanc, we've decided to give you a probationary license, to ride here at Texas Downs, however, any funny stuff and that's it. Do we understand one another?"

"Yes sir, I do, and thank you." Joe then turned, walking toward the door the three said, almost in unison, "Good luck, Joe Leblanc."

"Thanks," is what Joseph said, but he was thinking boy, if they only knew the trouble that was headed for their track, well, they would've run him out of town for sure!

What Joseph didn't know was that the stewards had received two phone calls, only minutes before he had walked into their office from the F.B.I. and the Texas Department of Safety, commonly known as the Texas Rangers. They were given very stiff instructions that Joseph Leblanc, be granted permission to ride, which they had done.

"Well, Brian, let's hit the stable area," Joseph said.

"While y'all do that, me and Lisa Marie, are gonna have some coffee in the track kitchen," Charlie told his son.

"Okay, Dad," Joe said as he kissed his wife on the cheek, then Jockey and agent went to the stable area to offer the services of jockey extrordinair, Joseph Leblanc.

Mean while, sitting at a table, Charlie and Lisa Marie were sipping on their coffee. "Charlie, it sure is good to be back around you, and it does my heart good to see you and Joe getting along so well," Lisa Marie told her father-in-law.

"Lisa, I should have known something was being held over my sons, head. It's just not in Joe, to cheat."

"Do you think that these people, have made a lot of money through the years having Joe, lose, on what should have been winners?" she asked, taking another sip of coffee.

"I don't know if they have or not. One thing does stick out in my mind though."

"Whats that?"

"Well, nobody has spoken a word about money, it's almost like money is secondary to them. Kinda makes it look like revenge."

"That's what I don't know Lisa, I just don't know," Charlie said as his still sharp mind went back to work.

Which left Lisa with thoughts of her own, like were her children okay, were they hungry.

Charlie reading her mind by the expression on her face said, "Now, now, it's going to be alright, them children are with their grandmama and she's not going to let anyone hurt them."

Lisa knew Maggie Leblanc, she knew her well, for she had spent more time at the Leblanc's home, than she did her own. It was almost like she had never moved out after her mother had bought their own home.

Maggie had been her second mom, she loved her very much, and Lisa knew if Maggie was able, she would take care of the children. She just didn't know what kind of shape her mother-in-law was in herself.

"Lisa, let's go watch a few horses train whadaya say?" Charlie asked.

"Sounds good, Charlie." As they got up from the table she asked, "How's this freak, going to get in touch with us?"

"I got a feeling that we want have to look him up. Don't worry, if he's bird doggin' us like he has been, he most likely knows the amount of sugar you put in your coffee."

Russo, meanwhile, had not gone to the track that morning. He needed a little time to bug both rooms, which had been easy enough. He now lay stretched out on his bed thinking about the suspects that could be behind all of this. Actually, he was drawing a big blank. This was the hardest case, he had worked on in a very long time. While he mulled these thoughts through his brain, his cell phone began ringing. "Hello, Russo here."

"Boss, it's me, David Pearce."

"Whadaya got, Dave?" Russo asked, almost impatiently.

"We have a boot print."

"That's it, a boot print," Russo returned.

"A very special print, boss, this particular boot is made by a company out of Laurel, Maryland."

"So!"

"Only jockey's or exercise riders use these boots."

"Where did you find this print?" Russo asked.

"Right out by the front door," Agent Pearce replied.

"So he did come through the front door, how did he do that without anyone hearing him? Given the fact there was no forced entry."

"Looks like he either picked it or had a key," Pearce said.

"So you guys checked all the windows, so there's no chance that he came through that way, is there?"

"I don't think so, besides the print was headed away from the house."

"That only means that he left the house through the front door."

"You've gotta point, Boss," returned Pearce.

"Well, stay on it David, and I'll be in touch." Russo, not waiting for Pearce's good bye, ended the call.

Damn it all to hell, this just keeps getting better and better.

Taking out a sheet of paper from his briefcase he scanned over his notes that he had taken thus far, and to them added Leblanc Children Kidnaping, must be someone they know, and left the house willingly, kidnapper is someone that works with horses. "Boy, that narrows it down," he said, aloud.

Mean while, back in the racing office, the clerks were busy taking entries for day after tomorrow's races. Brian had known quite a few trainers on the backside and a whole bunch remembered Joe Leblanc, his credentials spoke for themself, unfortunately, so did his past. But as luck and fate would have it, Johnny Wade's regular rider had broken his hand in a morning workout when he was thrown from his mount leaving the starting gate. At any rate, he needed a jockey for tonight's races on two of his horses and was willing to give Joe the chance.

He had remembered how good, a rider, Joe use to be, also he remembered the funny crap, and had stated. "You stiff one of my horses, Joe Leblanc, and I'll break your neck, do we understand one another?"

"Not a problem, Mr.Wade, I hope we can continue doing business," Joe had told him.

"See ya tonight then, I'll name you on both horses. The one in the second has a shot to win, the filly in the fifth, I just don't know, you look at the form Joe, see what you think."

And then the Hoss Cartright,look a like, turned and walked away.

Besides the two that Joe would ride tonight, he had picked up three others for tomorrow night.

Joseph was thinking about how Brian had conducted himself with the trainers, Joe had been around a lot of agents in his time and just like all jockey's have their opinions about agents, so did Joe, he thought there were two kinds, good ones and leaches. But he saw a little promise in Brian, at least down here in Texas.

Brian and Joe had caught up with Charlie and Lisa. And as they drove out of the stable area in Brians Chrysler, the Public Address system announced, that Joseph Leblanc had a message at the stable gate. "I'll bet I know who that is," Joe said.

"You want get any money off of me on that one," Charlie returned.

Jumping from the car, Joe went to retrieve the message.

Upon returning, Lisa Marie asked. "Who's it from?"

"Doesn't say, the caller asked the guard to tell me to check my messages at the front desk of our motel."

"Well, let's go see what it is," Charlie said impatiently.

On the short drive to the motel, Charlie asked, "So how's business going to be, Joseph?"

"I don't believe mounts will be a problem, the problems going to come with what the Headless Horseman want's me to do with them." Joe answered as Brian pulled up to the front office of the motel.

"I'll be right back," Joe said as he stepped from the vehicle.

He came back carrying a small box, as he got in, Lisa Marie asked. "What in the hell is that Joseph?" No one said it but each in the back of their minds was hoping that there was not some body part such as a finger or toe.

"Open it, Joseph!" Charlie said, before his imagination got to far out of hand.

"I am Dad, Jesus!" As Joe opened it, but before he could see what it was, it began ringing. "Goddam it!" Joe said as Lisa Marie said, "Jesus Christ!!"

Charlie even jumped a little.

Joseph finished unwrapping the paper that held the cell phone, finally he had it in hand. "Hello, hello!" He said, laughter is all he could hear and then, "Did that quicken the pace for ya, Joseph? No need to answer, I saw the way you jumped. That's right Leblanc, I'm close, real close. What if anything, do you ride tonight? The Headless Horseman asked.

"I ride the second and fifth," Joe answered.

"Good, Joseph, now the games begin. Does either have a shot to win?"

Looking at his wife and shaking his head answered. "The trainer likes the one in the second, doesn't know about the filly in the fifth."

"Here's the deal, I have in my possession thirty fingers and thirty toes. Tonight, the filly you ride in the fifth, if you win, for every length you win by I will let you talk to one of your children, one minute per length. If you run second, they want eat tonight, if you run third, your mother will lose a finger, for every length you lose the race by, good luck Joseph."

"You sick freak!" Joe yelled into the phone but it was in vain for the Headless Horseman had ended the call.

Joe quickly brought up the last incoming call and pressed send, that too was in vain for it had been either turned off or they wouldn't answer.

"Go to the room, Brian, now!" Joe told his agent.

"What's wrong Joe, what in the hell did he say?" Lisa Marie almost yelled.

"Just get to the room!" Joe told Brian again, which the agent did.

Once they were all in Joe and Lisa's room, Lisa Marie was the first one to speak. "Joseph, what did he say? I want you to tell me right now!"

"Everybody take a seat," Joe said, and then took a deep breath before continuing. "The rules have changed…"

"How do you mean?" Charlie broke in.

"Well, Dad, it's not about losing, anymore, it's about winning and the stakes are very high…"

Lisa Marie interrupted her husband this time. "Get the bush out of this conversation and tell us straight, what did he say?"

As Joe explained the rules, Agent Russo listened through the bug he had planted in their room.

He couldn't believe what he was hearing, he now knew above all, this was not about money. This was one very disturbed person.

After listening to what Joe had to say, Charlie reached for the racing form that was on the dresser. Handing it to his son, he asked. "Joseph, I only want to know one thing, can you win the damn race or not?"

"I don't know, but let's take a look at what her form say's. Joseph quickly turned to the past performances of Texas Downs, after getting to the fifth race he looked up the Johnny Wade trained filly, her name being Shesacutie, her last race, for the same price, she ran fifth. In that race, the distance was the same also, three quarters of a mile. She got beat a total of eleven lengths. "It doesn't look good,

Dad," Joseph told his father while he still looked over the filly's past performances.

"I will say this though," he continued. "It looks like they may have been riding her wrong. Look at this, Dad." Charlie came over to the desk where Joe sat.

"What is it, Joe?" Charlie asked.

"You see, in most races where the pace is fast she goes to the front and then she can't hold the pace, so she backs up. I'm just wonderin'..."

"I see exactly where you're going with it," Charlie said, almost smiling.

"When I go to the front, most of em will think I'm sett'n a fast pace that will back up, but in reality, I've got the speed backed up where I want it. So when they come to me, instead of dropping back, let her out a notch."

"That'll work, son, but two things have to happen. First, you gotta count on the other riders read'n the form, number two, their clock has to be wrong," Charlie told his son, and then added, "I have faith that you can get it done, though."

"Thanks, Dad, I've rode under pressure before, but nothing like this," Joe said.

"Joe, you gotta get some rest for tonight," Lisa Marie said.

"I would say that's our cue, Brian," Charlie said.

"I think you're right Charlie, I need to go back to the track to see about the draw. Do you wanta go with me?" Brian asked.

"Nah, I need some rest myself." And with that Charlie walked toward the door, with Brian already there and saying. "I'll pick you up jock, about five, post time for the first is at seven."

"I'll be ready," Joe answered, as Brian and his dad left the room.

"Joseph, how long do you think it's going to be before we get the kids and your mother back?" Lisa Marie asked her husband while she pulled back the blankets on the bed.

"To be honest, I just don't know." At least that's what he told his wife. What he was almost sure of though was that if they did get them back, it wouldn't be because the crazy bastard gave them back, it would be because they took them back.

Meanwhile, the motor home had been parked behind another old barn in Selma, Texas about four miles from where the race track was at.

"Grandma, why want this man let us go?" asked Bradly.

"Baby, I don't know other than he's gone crazy," she answered her grandson.

Right then someone was unlocking the door to the back room of the R.V. where the three were still being held.

"Now y'all don't say anything to provoke him, let me do the talkin'. Okay?"

"Okay, Grandmom, but we're hungry," Lanette said.

That in itself was breaking Maggie Leblanc's heart. She didn't care about herself, but she couldn't stand to watch her grandchildren suffer. It was the man that Maggie knew, he was the only one she ever saw, except for who was in the motor home when it had been parked in the Wal-Mart parking lot, the day they had nabbed her. But try as she might she just couldn't bring up the other person's face.

"My grandchildren are hungry, when are you going to feed them? The only thing you've given us is water and a bag of chips."

"I'll tell you what Maggie, I've just made a deal with Joseph, about yall's eating habits."

"What kind of deal?" Maggie asked.

"One he can't refuse," the man answered, in a bad imitation of Marlon Brando.

"When my dad catches you, he's gonna whoop the hell out of you, did you know that? You freak!" Lanette said.

"He already whooped his rear end, a long time ago," Maggie told her granddaughter.

"Shut up, both of ya, yakin' ass women. All the time want'n to run that mouth," the man told them, and then before leaving added, "You better hope he win's the fifth, as a matter of fact, you better start pray'n he does." And then the man walked out locking the door.

Those word's rang in Maggie's ears, just what did this maniac, have in store for them. And win the fifth, the fifth, at what track. She didn't even know where they were at. She knew that they had traveled all night, however she didn't know in what direction they had gone.

"Come on, kids, let's close our eyes and try to sleep. And when we wake up we'll have something to eat." She doubted if any of them could sleep, but she just didn't know what else to do. For the first time in her life, she was truly scared.

A few hours later, Joseph was getting dressed after waking up from his nap, he felt a little better, but he wanted to get to the jock's room a little early so that he could get in the sweat box. His weight was okay, he thought, however the sauna would get him loosened up a bit. Picking up the phone, he punched in his father's room. After three rings, "Hello," his father spoke into the phone.

"Dad, it's me Joe, is Brian about ready?"

"He just stepped outside, I think that Tracy called and he wanted a little privacy."

"Alright, I'll catch him before he goes back inside, I'm going to have him take me to the track. Dad, I'm leaving the cell phone that the Headless Horseman gave us with Lisa," Joe told his father.

"Sounds good Joseph, good luck tonight," Charlie said.

"Dad, you just might want to load up on a win ticket on that filly in the fifth and the other horse too. If it's winning, the Headless Horseman wants, well, the more I win, the better horses I'll ride."

"I see what you mean, Joe, and you're right," his dad told him.

Charlie knew his son was right about that, it can be like a domino effect. When your hot, you do get the best, on the other hand when your not your not. That's self explanatory.

"Anyway, don't forget Lisa, on your way over to the track."

After hanging up Joe kissed his wife and then stepped through the door to find Brian.

Agent Russo had been listening to the bug again up until Joseph left. And was now thinking about the whole scenario but nothing made sense, at first the Headless Horseman wanted Joe to lose, now he want's him to win. What was the motive, if not money.

The one thing that he did know was that he wouldn't rest until he found out who was behind this, he wanted justice for Agent Conner. He would have it at any cost.

Post time for the second race was twenty seven minutes away, Joe was ready. The only thing he waited for now was the call to the paddock, by the clerk of scales.

Joseph didn't know many rider's, although most knew who he was by reputation both good and bad.

"Riders, to the paddock," barked the clerk of scales.

Walking up to the trainer, of his mount, Mr. Wade held out his hand for the shake. "Hello, Joe," he said.

"Hello, Mr. Wade, how are ya?"

"I'm good, Joe, now look, this horse here need's a lot of warming up…"

Oh no, Joe thought, those words "need a lot of warning up" mean sore horse.

The trainer continuing on, "He likes to come from about three or four out of it and to the outside, if you get stuck down on the fence, he'll quit on ya."

"Yes sir, Mr. Wade, I've got it," Joe told the man with sincerity.

"Riders up," was announced, and then Joseph was legged up on a colt named Diamond Jim.

After warming up considerably Joe decided that Johnny Wade was right, the horse was alright, just a little stiff, but he seemed to have worked it out.

Joe had drawn the eight hole in a nine horse field, meaning he wouldn't have a lot of time to sit, which was good.

The assistant starter took his mount from the pony girl named Jan, who had wished him good luck.

"One back, boss!" One of the assistants shouted.

"Locked up!!!" Bam—and they were off and running down the backside.

Joe had gotten away good, and was now laying fifth about five lengths off the leaders and about two off the rail. He figured he was in good shape as they nailed the first quarter in twenty three, not bad Joe thought for a bunch of cheap horses. Moving into the turn he picked one up and was now in fourth place still two off the rail. This isn't going to be a problem he thought as he moved to the outside just a notch and picked off another one, he still felt like he had some horse left, at least he better. With less than an eighth of a mile to go, Joe went ahead and swung wide of the leaders, and then he went to work. The colt easily won by two and half lengths.

The only thought in Joe's mind was that if this were the filly race, he would have just won two and a half minutes of talk time with his children.

Meanwhile, in the grandstand, Charlie and Lisa Marie had both been watching on one of the many television screens through out the betting structure.

"Joe was right in telling me to bet on this horse, I just pray that he wins his next race by at least this many, Charlie was saying, to Lisa Marie.

"Me, too, Charlie," she said as the cell phone began to ring, both of them looking at each other.

"Well, answer it, Lisa."

Answering it she said, "Hello."

"Don't be shy, I saw the hesitation…" The voice said as Lisa began looking in every direction.

"Don't worry, Joe looks to be in good form. I'll tell you, though, I kind of hope he doesn't win on the filly, I believe I could have a lot of fun." Click the call was ended.

"It doesn't matter, Charlie," she told her father-in-law. And then added, "Let's go cash those tickets in."

"We're not cash'n we're bett'n it all back on the filly," Charlie said.

In the jocks quarters, Joseph was met with some congratulations for winning his first race at Texas Downs. He was thinking to himself that these riders didn't seem like a bad bunch. At least there didn't seem to be any Kami Kazis, so to speak.

He had a little time between his races so he once again took out the racing form to gander at the time fractions of the other horses that were in against the filly. He wanted to know just what they were capable of. On another note he was wondering how much money his father had bet on his winning ride in the second. But more than anything he was trying to keep his mind occupied as to not start dwelling on his children and what trauma they might be being subjected to.

Agent Russo was scanning the grandstand, hoping to spot something askew. He knew that the Headless Horseman was here, he could tell by the way Lisa Marie acted, while talking on the phone, she had suddenly spun in all directions. The caller had said something which really didn't matter, what was important was the fact that the bastard was here almost taunting them.

The Headless Horseman spotted the F.B.I. agent, he knew him from Rapid City. He had only seen him once, but that had been enough. What he needed to do was call home base and talk with his boss, which he did punching in a number. On the fourth ring it was answered. "Hello," the voice said.

"It's me, we need to talk…" He didn't finish what he had to say.

"I told you to never call me and especially here, you idiot!"

The voice was angry, very angry as they continued. "I'll be in touch!…". The call had ended.

"Damnit," he said, aloud, and then walked off knowing full well he had messed up.

"Riders, to the paddock," the jockey's were told.

Joe got up from where he had been sitting. He had been dreading this for what seemed an eternity. He didn't know whether he could win or not, although he was going to give it hell.

He had drawn the three hole, which meant he had to sit in there a little longer than the last one. He hoped she wasn't a nervous filly, that sure as hell wouldn't help matters.

Reaching the filly's saddling stall, he was again greeted by Johnny Wade.

"That was a fine race ridden on that colt, you think you could duplicate that?"

"We can sure try Mr. Wade, I'm going to try a little something with this filly."

"Whadaya mean?" Wade asked.

"Well, I'm going to the front as long as we can set a slow pace, I'm count'n on a couple of these guys not having a decent clock in their head." Joseph explained to the trainer what he had in mind.

"Well, you know a hell of a lot more about ride'n races than I do, so I'm just gonna give you the reins on this one, Joe."

"Riders up!" the official announced.

Legging Joseph Leblanc into the saddle Johnny Wade told his rider, "Good luck, Joe, have a safe trip."

The filly seemed alright to Joe, she was a dark bay with a little white on her right hind leg, and a star on her forehead. She stood not quite sixteen hands, she wasn't small by a long shot.

As they came on to the racing surface Joe looked at the tote board, which was discouraging, for the betting public had her odds of twelve to one. Joe knew that horses couldn't read odds, and jockey's shouldn't.

She warmed up good and she was on her toes, so when they headed for the starting gate, Joe felt almost confident.

In the grandstand there were two very nervous people, they had a lot more than just money at stake.

"Charlie, what do you really think? Can Joe win this damn race or not?" Lisa Marie asked, almost shaking.

"I don't know, but we're soon to find out," he answered his daughter-in-law.

The track announcer began. "They're all in line, the flag is up... And they're racing!"

Joe had made the lead just like he figured he would, what he hadn't counted on however was the apprentice rider that was out there wing dingin just to the inside and a half a length off of Joe. He had to make a decision and quick, should he give up the lead and try and make one run down the lane, or keep her live and try and make her last. Damn it, he thought, the hell with it.

He took hold and slowed her down letting the bug boy take the lead.

In the grandstand, Charlie Leblanc said, a loud. "God damn it, what's he doin'?"

As Joe checked to his inside he moved over on the rail, there was one horse on his outside running head and head with him. This is all wrong, these sons a bitches don't know whether there come'n or goin'. That's the thought he had as they entered the far turn, he was now in third place when he knew he had to make his move and as he started his drive, whip in hand, there all of a sudden was the five horse also moving up to challenge the leaders. And to Joe, it looked like the jock, on the five had a lot of horse left.

In the grandstand, Lisa Marie was damn near holding her breath, as her husband along with the five horse had over taken the leaders and were now head and head. Charlie Leblanc said aloud. "Damn it, Joe, go to work, son!!"

The announcer, himself, was wrapped up in the thrill of a stretch dual as he excitedly called the race. "Its Shesacutie and Devilerdue head and head, there stride for stride, it's not a battle, it's a war!!!"

Joe was pushing and pushing he had gone to a left handed stick but he couldn't shake loose from the five horse. That's when he decided to plug his filly in, he hadn't wanted to use the electrical device the size of a small bic lighter, known as a machine. But he was glad that he had carried it, he didn't know if she would even run from it. He took the shot and hit her with it zzz-zzz—it was working as she responded by digging deep and finding that winning gear, she shook loose of the filly beside her and surged to the lead as the announcer almost yelled.

"At the wire it's all Shesacutie by a length, with Devilerdue right there in second!!!" Joe had never felt such pressure as he had just then as he said, to himself. "Thank you, Lord, thank you!!!"

Lisa Marie had finally taken a breath and Charlie had to find a seat, he didn't know how much more his old heart could take.

At that moment the infamous cell phone rang, Lisa Marie answered on the second ring. "Hello!"

"Joseph did good, the Leblanc trio will have hamburgers and fries tonight. I also owe you one minute's worth of time to talk with your children, so I'll be in touch and remember I am watching you." The phone went dead.

"What did he say, Lisa?" Charlie asked, as he got back on his feet.

"He said, Joe did good." And as she explained the rest, Joseph was already back in the jock's room preparing for a quick shower. He was very anxious to get back to his wife.

The Headless Horseman, himself, went to cash his winning tickets, and while he stood in line another member of the Headless Horseman got in line also. "Do not turn around just keep looking at your program and listen to what I have to say. Do not ever call the number that you called earlier, when they want to speak to you, they will contact you. Is that clear? Only nod, if you understand, good." And then as fast as he had come, he was gone.

The man in line cursed silently to himself, who in the hell, did that guy think he was anyway? He knew the answer to that even before he had asked, what now seemed like the dumbest question ever.

Agent Russo had left the grandstand after the filly won her race. And was now sitting in the P.T. Cruiser, thinking how long could this go on, and what in the hell, is all this about? Money, greed, jealousy, what? He had no idea.

Sitting there waiting for the Leblanc's to emerge from the grandstand he saw the jock's agent Brian Gunn. Who was this guy really? He wanted to know more about him. In the morning he was calling the Bossier City office to get somebody over there to do a field check on this guy, have them go to the track and talk with some people that knew him, maybe talk to some of the riders, that he had represented. It wasn't much, but he had to start somewhere. He sure as hell wasn't getting anywhere like this. These were his thoughts as the Leblanc's, walked from the betting enclosure.

"So, he said, that they would eat, right?" Joe asked.

"Yes, Joseph, that's what he said," answered Lisa Marie.

After meeting with Brian as Agent Russo looked on, the Leblanc's got in Charlies pick-up and Brian in his car. Agent Russo on a shim decided that if they went in different directions he was going to follow Brian. Maybe it was just a hunch but it was something he felt he needed to do.

Sure enough at the exit, Brian turned left instead of following the Leblanc's, to the right. Russo dropped in three cars behind as not to be noticed. Then Brian turned left into the Shell station, Russo turned left also but continued on down the side street. At the next stop sign he turned around, and them pulled into the station. Brian was on the pay phone up against the wall of the station, and seemed not to pay attention.

"Now, now Joseph, don't go get'n uppity with me, but I do owe you, so would you like to talk with one or both children?" And Joseph, this is not a free for all call so to speak, there are rules. And if you break the rules or the kids break the rules, I will break something of my choice on either or both. You will ask simple questions or make simple statements, the children, have been instructed to answer only yes or no. Do you understand?"

"I understand, I want to talk, with both," Joe told the Headless Horseman.

"Very well, now tonight it's your turn, tomorrow night your wife will get the chance. Your on the clock,go."

"Hello, Lanette, Brad?"

"Yes," Lanette answered.

"We love you, honey. Are you okay?"

"Yes."

"Your mama and me we're going to get you back, God, we love you."

"Yes."

"Times up, Joseph. Now get ready for your next thirty seconds," the Headless Horseman said, adding, "Go."

"Brad, we love you, we're going to come for you, just hang in there little man."

"Yes."

"Is your grandmom okay?"

"Yes."

"Tell her we love her, me, your moth…"

"Time's up."

"Damn it," Joseph said.

"Oh, one other thing, read the headlines in the morning, it'll be a real eye opener for you!"

Then the phone call was ended leaving Joe to wonder what was going to be in the head lines tomorrow.

"How are they Joseph?" Lisa asked.

"They sound good. They're with Mom, he said, you'd have the chance to talk with them tomorrow," he told his wife as he put his arm around her and added, "It's going to be alright, baby, I promise."

Tears rolled down Lisa Maries cheeks as she buried her head into her husbands chest.

He himself, was replaying the conversation with the Headless Horseman, there was something that he said that didn't register, what in the hell was it?"

"Joseph," Charlie said.

"Yeah, Dad?"

"What did you do with the machine? It might need a tune up," his father asked.

"It's fine, Dad, I've got it back at the tra…: wait a minute, wait just a freakin minute!" Joe exclaimed as he held his wife back at arms length. And then went on. "The bastards either a rider, or he use to be a rider. He knew I used a machine on that filly, and not only that, the way he said it!"

"What in the hell are you talkin about Joseph?" His dad asked, rising from the chair where he had been sitting.

"Dad, he told me with those exact words, that it was a good thing, I plugged the filly in, then he went on to say thank God, for general electric."

"Are you sure?"

"Dad, I know what he said, and not only that, it's exactly what we would say, in the jock's room after a race back at Cajun Downs."

"You were pluggin horses in back then?" Charlie asked.

"Dad," Joseph said as it look like, his father had a big red balloon tied to his head.

"Never mind," Charlie returned.

"So, what your say'n, Joe, is that he's a jockey?" Lisa Marie said, and sort of asked at the same time.

"I don't think he rides anymore, because you talked to him right after I won on the filly," Joseph said.

"That's right. Joe, but that only means he didn't ride tonight," she told her husband.

Then Charlie cut in. "How about this, we know or at least he makes us think, that he had something to do with your daddy's murder."

"That's right, Dad, we're assuming that he's old enough for that to be true. Although it's not a hard core fact, maybe it's a magicians trick, what do they call it?"

Lisa Marie answered, "I believe it's called slight of hand, where the left hand get's your eyes occupied while the right hand steals you blind."

"That's good, Lisa," Charlie said.

"But now what? We aren't any closer to catching this guy, than we were ten minutes ago," Joe said as he yawned, then added, "I know this, though, tonight, Mom and the kids ate and that they are safe at least for the moment. This sick bastard wants to play games for awhile, giving us time to figure out who he is."

"That's what he's doing, playing with us," Lisa Marie said.

"Well, I'm goin' to bed, I've had all I can stand, and maybe I can rest a little easier, know'n that Maggie's okay and that she's with the children," Charlie told his daughter-in-law and son as he started for the door.

"Dad, tell Brian we need to be at the track by five thirty in the mornin', if it's winning that the Headless freak wants, well, I sure know how to do that."

"That you do, son, that's a fact," Charlie said as he crossed the room to give Tee Joe a hug and as he did, he said, "Joseph, I love you, do you know that?"

"Yeah, Dad, I do, I love you, too."

Then Charlie also hugged Lisa Marie saying, "You're a good woman, Lisa Marie, I always knew you were, and I love you for it."

"Thank you, Charlie, I love you, but then you know that, don't you!"

It wasn't a question, but a statement.

Charlie only shook his head, as he said, "Goodnight, y'all."

Both Lisa and Joe said, at the same time, "Goodnight, Dad."

Five o'clock came early but as soon as the wake up call came through, Joe's feet hit the floor. Lisa Marie was also awake, and had gotten up to plug in the coffee maker, while Joe got ready for the morning workouts at the track.

"Baby, call Brian to see if he's up yet, would you, please?" Joe called, from the bathroom.

"Already did. He's almost out the door," Lisa answered.

"Good," Joe said as he came from the bathroom, giving his wife a good morning kiss and taking the coffee cup she offered. He then picked up the phone as Lisa Marie asked. "Now, what are you doing?"

"I want Dad to come over while I'm at the track, at least I'll know that you're safe," Joseph told her just about the time someone knocked on the door.

"Who is it?" Joe asked.

"Brian and your dad," the voice said.

Opening the door Joe told the two, "Mornin'. Y'all, want some coffee?"

"I'll take some," Charlie said as he walked into the room.

"I'm gonna wait till we get to the track kitchen, but thanks anyway," Brian told Joe.

"Dad, you don't mind stay'n with Lisa, do ya?"

"Not at all, we don't need to be out there this early, do we Lisa?" Charlie said.

"I'm glad you feel that way Charlie, besides I wanna call Mom after while," Lisa told them.

"Damn, I'm sorry Lisa, I talked with her last night. She's fly'n in this afternoon. I meant to call you when I got back from the store, but it slipped my mind," Brian told Lisa.

"C'mon, Brian, we need to go," Joseph said as he kissed his wife and asked, "Y'all come'n later?"

"Meet ya in the kitchen at the break. I love you, Joe," she said.

"Love you, too," he told his wife, and then to his father said, "Take care of her, Dad."

"Go on, get outta here," Charlie told his son.

As Brian and Joseph were sitting in the kitchen sipp'n coffee, Johnny Wade pulled up a chair. "Morn'n fella's. Joe, that was nice ride'n last night, you're gonna shine around here you keep that up."

"Thanks, Mr. Wade," Joe said, and then asked, "Is there anything we can do for ya, this mornin'?"

"I've got a two-year-old colt to breeze about a quarter to nine, he's started one time, ran third. You can breeze him, if you want."

"Sounds good, Mr. Wade," Joe told the big man.

"You ready to make the rounds, Joe?" Brian asked.

"Yeah, I'm ready, let's do it," he told his agent, then turned to Johnny, telling him, "See ya, after while." And then Joseph and his agent walked from the kitchen to try and drum up some counts.

Back at the motel room, Charlie and Lisa were also having coffee, while they watched the morning news.

"So, Charlie, wada' ya think of Brian?" Lisa asked.

"I've known Brian for quite a while now. And I just don't know how to read the guy. He just never seems to hit his stride."

"I know what ya mean," she said when a breaking news story flashed on the news.

"Turn that up Lisa," Charlie said since she had the remote.

A woman news reporter was standing in what looked like a super market parking lot and was saying, "Late, last night, as this grocery store in Selma closed, manager Susan Hernandez found a man slumped over his steering wheel, upon approaching to see if he was alright, Ms. Hernandez, noticed the man bleeding. That's when she used her cell phone to call 911. The victim of an apparent robbery, the man was pronounced dead at the scene. If anyone has any information concerning this crime, please contact the Selma Police Dept. Now, back to you Dan."

At that moment, someone, knocked on the motel room door.

"Surely that's not the maid." Lisa got up to answer. "Who is it?"

"Mrs. Leblanc?" a man's voice asked.

"Yes," she answered, looking through the peep hole in the door.

"It's David Pearce, we met at your mother's," Pearce told her through the door.

"Of course, I'm sorry," Lisa said as she unlocked the door and greeted him. "So, Mr. Pearce, what can we do for the F.B.I. this morning?"

"May I come in Mrs. Leblanc?"

"By all means, Charlie, this is agent David Pearce. He was at mom's the morning after the kids were taken, Mr. Pearce, my father-in-law, Charlie Leblanc."

"Mr. Leblanc," said, the agent, offering his hand.

Extending his hand also, Charlie asked. "What can we do for you? Or do you have some news, that you know who took my wife and grand kids?"

"No sir, we don't have anything concrete at this time except for the fact that another agent was killed last night."

"And what bearing does that have on us Mr. Pearce?" Lisa Marie asked.

"For one thing, he was the lead investigator on the Headless Horseman case and we have reason to believe that his death is directly related to that case."

"You're telling us that the agent killed, was Russo?" Charlie asked, as he sat back down, he was thinking, Jesus, where's this going to end. But then he really didn't want to know the answer to that question, just thinking about it made him wince.

"That's right, Mr. Leblanc, the local police seem to think it was a robbery, and that's what we want them to keep believing. However, the killer didn't know that Agent Russo was a stickler on notes, as a matter of fact he had a small recorder that he kept with him at all times. We're having it analyzed to see what may be pertinate to this case, it's also possible that his dying words are on that tape." As Agent Pearce explained these things, Lisa, sat down and motioned for the agent to do the same. After sitting down he took a deep breath and started again, "Look, I realize that both of you, along with your husband, have been through a tremendous ordeal…"

Pearce was interrupted. "Agent Pearce, we're not through it, we're living it every minute of every day, can you even start to understand the pressure that we are under?" Lisa Marie said.

"No, Mrs. Leblanc, I can't but understand even though I worked with Mr. Russo on many things, on this I'm kind of in the dark."

Standing up, Charlie said, "Well then, Mr. Pearce, let me help you a little, this Headless Horseman bastard doesn't want the F.B.I. around us. Maybe that's what got Russo killed, I don't know. I do know this much, just you bein' here put's my wife and grandchildren in more danger than they're already in. So I suggest that you go listen to Russo's tape, and if I were you, I'd make damn sure that I didn't do whatever he did to get himself killed. Now me and my daughter-in-law need to get over to the track, if you don't mind."

"No, sir, I want hold you up anymore than I already have. Please forgive me."

"Mr. Pearce, there's nothing to forgive. We're just tryin' real hard to not get our loved ones killed. Surely you can understand that." Lisa Marie told the F.B.I. agent.

Standing up himself, he took out two cards with his number on them and handing one to each Leblanc and said, "We want be far, we'll try and stay out of sight. However, if you need me for anything please call me." And then opening the door to leave, Lisa Marie said, "Mr. Pearce."

Turning, the agent, responded, "Yes, ma'am."

"I'm sorry about Agent Russo."

"I am too, Mrs. Leblanc, I am too." Then he turned and walked through the door.

Meanwhile, over at Texas Downs, Joe had breezed three horses and still had one to go before the break. He and Brian had also talked with the trainers of the horses he would ride tonight, there were three, two had a shot at winning, the third one was a first time starter, that was anybody's guess.

Danny Roller trained the colt in the first race, while Teresa Sanchez trained the first time starter in the sixth, that race was going five and half furlongs. The other horse that Joe was to ride, was in the ninth and final race of the evening and was trained by Martin Brady.

Walking into barn fourteen, Joe looked up at the exercise rider on the big bay horse that was going around the shedrow, turning to his agent, he said, "I know that guy."

The exercise rider spoke up. "Yeah, Leblanc, you know me, you just can't put a finger on it, can ya?" And then urging his mount to continue he rounded the corner and was out of sight

"Who was that Joe?" Brian asked.

"I think it was this guy that use to ride around Jersey, I'm try'n to remember his name, Billy, that's it, Billy Cox."

"Sounds like he's got an attitude toward you," Brian told Joe.

"I got an attitude alright," Billy said as he came back around the corner.

"Remember Tad Inman, don't you Joe? When he moved from Jersey to New York, I was gonna ride for him until the great Joseph Leblanc offered his services. Do you know where I wound up ride'n after that?" Billy Cox asked.

"I haven't got a clue, Billy," Tee Joe answered.

"Oklahoma, that's where. At a place where the purses are so cheap you gotta win three or four a week just to keep your head above water. And then I broke my leg and when it was over, by the time I could ride races again I was way to big."

"And you blame my ass, for all that? You can't be serious," Joe told the man, who just shrugged and walked away.

"C'mon, Joe,we have to hurry," Brian said, and then leading the way down the shedrow, where Don Vanhoughton waited to have his horse breezed by Joe Leblanc.

Sitting in the track kitchen, pulled up to a table, the three Leblanc's and Brian Gunn were having coffee, with Lisa Marie replaying the conversation that Charlie and her had earlier with F.B.I. Agent David Pearce.

"Was this Pearce guy sure Russo was killed by the Headless Horseman?" asked Joe.

"He said, they were pretty sure, but they have a cassette from a mini recorder that Russo always carried with him. Most likely it could have Russo's dying words on it, at least that's what Pearce thinks," Lisa Marie explained.

"This is getting crazier and crazier," Brain said and, then standing, added, "Joe, I'm going into the racing office and check entries, I'll meet you back here after you breeze that horse for Johnny Wade, how's that sound?"

"Sounds great, get us on some live ones," Joe told his agent whom he was starting to like.

After Brian walked off Joe was the first to speak. "Well, have you heard from dickhead, today?"

"Not yet, which I'm kind of glad he didn't call while Agent Pearce was at the room," Lisa said.

"I've got something interesting," Joe said as to took another sip of his coffee. "I ran into a guy that use to ride back in Jersey. I recognized him earlier while he was on a horse. He's blaming me for some crap that happened back when I was still an apprentice."

"Really, Joe, what did he say?" asked Charlie.

While Joseph explained his encounter with Billy Cox, his wife and father listened intently. When he was finished his dad asked. "Do you think he's the one, Joseph?"

"I don't know, Dad, but I think we should get that Agent Pearce to at least run a check on him, he's been carrying a lot of anger around for a long time."

"How old is he Joe?" asked Lisa.

"Not old enough to have been around when your dad was killed, he might be forty-five at the most," Joseph answered.

That's when Charlie cut in. "Yeah, Joe, but what were we talk'n about last night, remember? Maybe he just wants us to believe he had something to do with Gerard's death."

"Yeah, you gotta point, Dad, seems like we keep hit'n dead ends. But I gotta get back to work, I got one to breeze for John Wade. The guy I won those two races for last night. I'd be will'n to bet, he's never won two races in one night before, you'd think I was the greatest thing since sliced bread."

"You didn't know that Joseph?" His wife kidded, as she smiled at her husband, all the while thinking just how much she loved Joseph Leblanc, and how much she missed her children.

"Yeah, yeah, I'll meet y'all back here in about thirty minutes," Joe said as he stood, kissed Lisa Marie and patted his dad on the back.

After Joe had gone Charlie told Lisa Marie, "Why don't you call Pearce and give him Billy Cox's name, see what he comes up with."

"Sounds good, Charlie," she said as she punched Pearce's number into the cell phone that the Headless Horseman gave them. "You think dickhead, will mind if we use his phone to call the F.B.I.?" Lisa said, with a smile.

"I hope not, Lisa Marie," answered Charlie as he took another drink of coffee.

When Lisa was finished with the call, she said to Charlie. "Well, he said he would run it but first he'd have to get in touch with the licensing office here so that he could get his social security number."

"Good, Lisa, at least it makes you think somebody's doing something," Charlie replied, to his daughter-in-law as he finished off the coffee he had been nursing, then said, "Let's go see what's going on in the racing office." And with that, Lisa and Charlie walked away from the table.

Meanwhile there was a telephone conversation taking place between two Headless Horsemen members, one of them was in the motor home the other was on a pay phone at the racetrack.

"You dumb little bastard, you killed an F.B.I. agent, in a super market parking lot, and then didn't search the vehicle to see if he had any evidence on us!" The pay phone man said.

"But he needed killin', he was getin' close to us. I did the right thing!" The man in the motor home said.

"You may be right about that, but damn'it he had a recorder in the car."

"He did?"

"Yeah, and not only that, it may have been on when he was killed. You didn't say anything that would incriminate us, did you?"

"I don't think I said anything at all and neither did he."

"Well I gotta go, you just make the call to the cat in the bag, as planned, give him the instructions for tonight. Then you lay low, do you understand?"

"I got it, don't worry, alright." There was no use waiting for an answer the line was already dead.

"Arrogant asshole," he said to himself. Then he went back to check on the little Leblanc flock.

Joseph had met back up with his wife and dad in the racing office where the clerks were busy taking entries.

"Joe, I called that guy Pearce, about running a check on Billy Cox, I'm supposed to call him back this afternoon to see what he found out, if anything." Lisa told her husband as the three walked outside.

"That's good Lisa, I'm glad you thought of it." Joe returned just about the time their cell phone beckoned to be answered.

Lisa handing it to her husband said. "I'm sure this is for you."

Joe answered on the fourth ring. "Hello," he said into the phone.

"Hello, Joseph, what do you ride tonight? Never mind I already know. Tonight on Danny Roller's horse in the first I want you to win, however that's not all, there is a girl rider, her name is Amanda Davis. She rides one in the first also, she will run second to you, are you following me so far? Good, now listen closely this is where it starts getting good, you see last night was more or less a what you might want to call…trial run so to speak. Now comes the real challenge. Tonight, not me, but you, have three bodies to bet, with each body represents one chip. Minimum bet is one chip. Do you understand the game? Do you know what it means?"

Answering, Joe offered a weak. "Yes, I know what it means."

"Good, Joe, now here we go. I'm betting that you can't make the first race finish with you winning and the girl placing second, your bet, Joe."

Joe didn't know what to do, but was a little unclear about the betting so he had to ask. "Okay, say I bet one chip and I win, just what do I win?"

"It's simple Joseph, you win a chip. In reality, you have won a body. So now, instead of three chips you now have four. But when you lose a chip, it's gone. This is the deal, you win all my chips then there will be one grand finale! If you win that, then you get to trade your chips in. And Joe, this is not one of those deals where you pitch till you win. Know what I mean? Your time is limited, one week from tonight and game is finished. So what's tonights bet in the first?' he asked Joseph.

Joe's mind was just about to explode, so many things were running through it. He didn't know how he could possibly bet like this?

"Joseph, I'm waiting," the Headless Horseman said.

"I'm thinking, damn it! Okay, okay, look, I'll bet the minimum, one chip."

"That's it Joe, play it safe. There was a time when you hadn't been so safe, at least with other peoples lives. But at any rate welcome to the game, and Joe?"

"Yeah?"

"Good luck racing!" Then the call was ended.

By the look on Joe's face Lisa Marie knew that whatever he was going to say would not be good. She almost wished that she could freeze time so that she wouldn't have to hear it, but even though she knew this, she still had to know. "Joe, what did he say? What does he want you to do this time?"

As he explained how the game would be played, his wife and father looked on in disbelief, and when he finished, tears were rolling down Lisa Marie's cheeks as she thought of the hell that her children were being subjected to.

Charlie himself only shook his head and then under his breath said, "I'm gonna kill this bastard if it's the last thing I do."

At just about the moment they reached Charlie's truck Brian caught up with them.

"Hey, where y'all goin'?" he asked.

"Back to the motel, I need to study the racing form for tonights races and get some rest," Joseph told his agent.

"Well, I picked up another horse for you to ride tomorrow night," Brian told Joe.

"So how many do I ride tomorrow night?" Joe asked.

"You ride six, business is really picking up," Brian said, and then almost as an after thought he added, "Lisa, I go to pick your mother up from the airport at about three, do you want to come with me?"

"No, I don't think so, I want to hang with my husband as much as I can before he has to go ride," she answered.

"Brian, since Tracy's coming in, I'll get another room so y'all can have some privacy," Charlie said.

"No way, Dad, you're not stayin' by yourself! You're moving right on over with me and Lisa Marie," Joe said.

"Joe, I can't…"

"Oh yes, you are Charlie, consider it settled!" Lisa Marie said.

"I'll see y'all later then, okay?" Brian told them.

Twenty minutes later Joe and Lisa were sitting in their motel room, Joe was deeply engrossed in the racing form and he figured he had a pretty good chance of winning the first race, the real problem was, the horse that Amanda was on. She had ridden the horse in his last five starts, and he was starting to pick up on something.

Every time she rode him she would break with the pack but she would always go to the front, she'd set a blistering pace going the first quarter in twenty two flat, the half in forty four and then finish up six furlongs in one thirteen and change. She just couldn't keep the pace and so they would run past her down the lane.

Joe also looked at some other races that Amanda had ridden. She sent damn near everything to the front and damn near everything finished at the back of the pack. Joe wanted to see the replays of some of the races she had ridden in.

Charlie had come into the room while Joe had been studying the form and was talking with Lisa Marie when Joe said, "Dad, Lisa, let's go to the track, I want to watch some films of this girl rider, Amanda."

"Did you find something that might help?" Charlie said, with enthusiasm.

"I may have, but I'll have to see the tapes first," he told his father.

"Well, lets go see!" Lisa Marie told the two men.

Meanwhile, Agent Pearce was going over the tape that they had retrieved from Russo's car, and also some other things as well, that they had discovered in his motel room.

The tape was mostly a rundown of what Pearce already knew. The one thing that Russo had said as he died, and the way he said it, made Pearce feel like there was an underlying statement. Russo had said, "So it wasn't Brian Gunn after all." That was it, that was all he had said as he died. Had he known who the killer was? Pearce after pausing to think about it for a moment or so, said to himself, "Naw, he would of said who, if he had known." The tape, however, had continued to play, Russo had turned it on, but didn't turn it off before he had died. Listening now, to the silence of the tape, he thought he had heard something in the background, as he rewound the tape, then he pushed play, there it was again, somebody had said something. What did they say, after rewinding again he turned the volume up as high as it would go.

At the track Joe thought he had found out the flaw in the girls riding ability, or at least some of it.

Now what he needed to do was find out where she was at now. So the trio headed over to the racing office to get her agents number.

Which they found easy enough. Joe wanting to keep the cell phone clear just in case the crazy bastard wanted to call, he popped two quarters into the pay phone and dialed the number.

"Hello," the voice said on the other end.

"Hi, this is Joe Leblanc. Is this Mike Hayes?"

"Sure is. What can I do for ya."

"Well, I'm trying to get in touch with Amanda Davis."

"May I ask what for?"

"Well, Mike, I know this may sound a little crazy, but I'd actually like to help her out with her riding. Just a little."

"You're right, it does sound crazy. Let me ask you a question."

"Sure, go ahead," Joe said.

"Why would you want to help her? That's all I want to know."

"Would you give me the number if I told you that if I could get her to ride a little better that it would help me out tremendously," Joseph told the man.

"I have no idea what in the hell you're talk'n about, but if you want to help her, or you think you can, then by all means call her. Here's the number.

After ending the call with the confused agent, he dialed Amanda's cell phone number. After explaining that it was important that he talk to her in person before the races. She agreed to meet him at the track in the parking lot at five thirty, an hour and a half prior to the first race.

Joseph was not the only one getting thing's done. Agent Pearce had gotten some information back on Billy Cox. The tape had also been sent to the lab, try as he might, he couldn't make out the words the killer had spoken, as he exited Russo's P.T. Cruiser. He was in hopes that the lab technician could amplify it.

As for Mr. Cox, he had certainly been around, he also had had his brushes with the law. However, in the last five years his record was clean. Which only meant that he hadn't been caught. Pearce wanted to look a little deeper into the activities of Billy Cox, which prompted his next phone call.

Brian had picked Lisa Maries mother up from the airport and they were now on their way to the motel. "So Brian, how's Joe doing?" Tracy asked her husband.

"He rode his ass off last night, made a big impression on the trainers and tonight, I've got a feeling he's gonna do good again."

"Well, I hope so. You see, Brian, I told you a long time ago that Joe Leblanc was a sensational rider, or at least he was before his so-called fall from grace."

"You were right, as always, my dear."

"And Lisa Marie, how's she been holding up under all of this?"

"I think it's starting to get to her, but sometimes it's hard to tell just what she's thinking," Brian said.

"I know what you mean, Brian," Tracy said as she reached over to take her husband's hand.

The Leblanc trio were now sitting in the parking lot waiting on Amanda to show up. Joe had studied and re-studied the charts of the races that he would ride tonight. He knew exactly how he was going to ride the horse in the first race, he also knew what to tell Amanda.

Pulling into the parking lot in her Ford Mustang, she parked, got out and upon seeing Joe, she walked over. "Hello, Joe, right?"

"That's right, Amanda, this is my wife and my dad," Joe said, introducing them.

"So what's this all about?" she asked.

"Well, I don't want you to get the wrong idea Amanda, however, I think I can help your riding a little," Joseph told her.

"You don't like my riding?" she asked, a little miffed.

"It's not that, it's just I think you can do better."

"And why would you want to help me? You don't even know me."

"I know it sound's crazy but, aw the hell with it. I'm gonna tell you something. I hope then you can understand that we need your help," he told the now totally confused Amanda Davis.

Speaking up, Lisa said, "Joe, why don't you let me handle this?"

"Go ahead, you've got the floor," he told Lisa, with relief in his voice.

"Amanda, let's you and me take a little walk." Lisa Marie said, while the two women were gone, Joe told his dad. "So what do you think? You think we can get this race, the way we want it?"

"Joseph, we've got a helluva lot ride'n on it, so I'd say, you damn well better, wouldn't you?"

"Yeah, Dad, I'm pretty sure I've got my end," Joseph answered.

Walking back up were the two women, with Lisa saying, "Joe, I kinda ran it down to her, the short version.

She want's to help."

"Great," said Joe.

"How do you think I should ride this horse in the first?" Amanda asked.

"Okay, here we go. Amanda, on a lot of your horses, that you ride, you always go to the front and set fast paces. What I want to know is, why?"

"I don't have enough lead in my ass, to slow 'em down..."

Interrupting, Joseph told her. "Exactly, Amanda, you want to know what I do when I want the horse to go on and pick it up?"

"Sure," she said.

"I pick up the bit, and when I want one to relax, I throw their heads away. In other words, I let 'em run on a loose rein, so here's what I want you to try tonight..."

Meanwhile, Agent Pearce was watching from a distance and thinking what in the hell are they doing. Was it possible that the Leblanc's, were behind this whole thing and that old lady Leblanc and the kids were at some motel in Disney Land? He doubted that very much. He wished that he had not been called in to handle this case, it smelled bad, real bad!

And there was yet another, that studied the meeting taking place in the parking lot. Pearce was not aware of him, although the Headless Horseman, was well aware of Pearce.

One hour later the jockey's that were to ride the first race were being called to the paddock.

"Amanda," Joe said, just before they walked out to the saddling paddock.

"Yeah, Joe," she replied.

"Just stay with me, when I go, you go. I want you to the inside of me and I'll pick the holes," Joe said to her.

Taking a breath and exhaling, she said, "Let's go."

He then added a somewhat nervous smile.

Danny Roller greeted Tee Joe Leblanc in the usual manner of a handshake between rider and trainer. "How you doin' tonight, Joe?"

"Pretty good, Danny, You doin' okay?"

"I'll be a lot better if we can win this one," the trainer answered.

"Danny, I'm pretty sure we can win it. I've been readin' the form. I don't think we can lose."

"I'm glad you feel that way," Danny said with a smile, just about the time the paddock official barked, "Riders up!"

Legging Tee Joe into the saddle, Danny said, "Good luck, Joe, have a safe trip." Tee Joe just nodded as he was led out to the pony horse that would take him to the starting gate.

Looking at the odds board, Joe thought to himself, there's going to be some pretty surprised people tonight.

Joe had the five hole and Amanda the two. As they warmed up their counts, Joe was scrutinizing the other seven horses not including Amanda. The horse that Joe was on, was named Texas Pete, Amanda's was Counter Strike.

As the assistant starters began loading horses into the starting gate. Amanda looked over at Joe, who nodded his head and smiled in such a way that if you could convert expressions into words, his smile would have said, "You can do it. I know you can."

"They're all in line," the track announcer said over the P.A. system, waiting for the break. "And they're racing down the backside, that's Texas Pete, in front, as he moves down on the fence. In second, that's Roadhouse, with Zip Bye, following up in third, tucked down on the rail is Counter Strike running fourth..."

Joe was wondering how Amanda was faring, at least he knew she wasn't in front burning her mount up. Now's the time to slow 'em down a little and as he did...

"Texas Pete, has given the lead away, as Roadhouse takes command, with Zip Bye, right there in third…"

Joe was just coasting as he checked under his left arm, and there she was, her horse looked to be running easy…

"As they enter the far turn, that's Roadhouse, in front," barked, the announcer and taking a breath continued, "Texas Pete, looks to be making a move as they approach the three-eights pole, that's Zip Bye, on the outside…

Joe could feel it, he knew it was time, and as he prayed that Amanda could go with him, he cocked his whip, and tapped his mount on the shoulder, the big bay responded.

The announcer, continued the call. "Spinning out of the turn, it's still Roadhouse, but here comes Texas Pete as he gun's down the leader…"

Joe had pushed his mount into the hole on the rail and as he started to check where Amanda was at, he heard. "I'm here, Joe go on!" And go on he did as he was now head to head with Roadhouse, and Joe was moving him over making a hole for Amanda to get through. The pressure was to much for Roadhouse, as he gave way to Texas Pete, who as soon as he was clear Joe moved over more so that he could throw a little dirt in Roadhouses face which completely discouraged the red gelding. The announcer, finished the call. "They're at the wire and it's all Texas Pete, in front followed by Counter Strike."

Two jumps later, Amanda and Joe were galloping their mounts out around the clubhouse turn. "Did you get up for second, Amanda?" Joe asked, as they started slowing their horses down.

"I sure did, that was awesome, the way you did that," Amanda told him.

Then turning their horses around and starting back to be unsaddled, Joe said to her. "Thank you, Amanda, I'll see ya back in the room." He then picked up the pace heading back for the win picture. All the while thinking, I wonder what this asshole, will want next.

Meanwhile up in the grandstand, Lisa Marie and Charlie were both letting out sighs of relief.

"Lisa, that boy can sure horseback," Charlie said, just about the time that their cell phone beckoned to be answered.

"Well, we know who that is," Lisa said as she answered timidly. "Hello."

"My, my, now that was truly, poetry in motion. Your husband did good. As a matter of fact, Joe and I have business later so stay close to the phone. And then having said that he ended the call.

"What did he say this time?" Charlie asked.

"He said, that Joe did good, and that they had business."

"I wonder what that'll be?"

"There's no tellin', Charlie, no tellin' at all,," Lisa answered.

That night Joe not only won the first race but also the last. The first time starter ran third, the colt needed the race to pump some air into him. Joe could tell though that he'd soon be a contender, for the colt was game, he had given all he had. Joe felt pretty confidant that Teresa would ride him back the next time the two year old ran.

After showering he got dressed and walked out of the jock's room to meet his wife and dad.

"So did you hear from the ass-hole, yet?" Joseph asked as he kissed his wife.

"Sure did, say's he's got some business for us," Lisa Marie answered.

"We might as well get to the motel before he calls, I don't want to be here at the track trying to talk with him, whatever he want's us to do," Joseph told them.

Once back in their motel room, the red button on the telephone indicating they had a message at the front desk was blinking.

"Surely, he wouldn't leave us a message," Lisa Marie said as she picked up the receiver to call the front desk.

"Joe, you looked in really good form tonight," Charlie told his son.

"Thanks, Dad, but I'll tell you who impressed me and that was Amanda. I watched the replay, I'd say she has a lot of potential."

"That was a message from Mom, telling me to check in with her when we got back from the track," Lisa told the two as she set the phone down.

"There he is," Charlie said as the cell phone began ringing.

"Well, here we go," said Joseph. Taking a breath, he answered the phone. "Hello."

"Joseph Leblanc, you were very impressive tonight, and so was the girl. Now you have four chips, however, you can trade one for one minute talk time with your children. Do you want to trade or wait?"

Joseph, answering, said, "So if I win two more plus the finallie, I get my mother and my children back, right?"

"That's right, you can bet one chip on the next race and even if you lose, you still have the original three. But if you bet two and you lose, somebody dies. Are we clear?"

"Crystal clear. Also, I don't want to trade chips for talk time."

"So what's the bet?" the Headless Horseman asked.

"I'll bet one."

"Now remember, Joseph, you only have six days left in which to win all my chips."

"I'm still betting one chip."

"Very well, play it as you will. Tomorrow night, I am betting that you can not win two out of the six you ride."

Interrupting the Headless Horseman, Joseph asked, "Is that it?"

Taking the lead back, the Headless Horseman replied, "Of course, that's not all, the girl Amanda, she will also win two, and you will specify which two that you will win. I'll call back in one hour for your answer." The phone call was ended.

"What does he want now Joseph?" Lisa Marie and Charlie both answered simultaneously.

"In short, he said get a form. He want's me to win two races out of the six that I ride tomorrow night. And I have to pick the winners," Joe told them as he started rifling through the racing form, and then added, "Oh, yeah, he want's Amanda to win two tomorrow night also."

130

"If you ride anything that's live, you could more than likely get it done," Charlie said, and then asked, "But what's Amanda ride?"

"That's what I'm looking at now. The first one she rides is in the third race, and she's picked to run second."

"What's the race look like?" Lisa Marie asked.

Answering Joseph said, "Well, the race itself, is a non-winner of two races ever for three year filly's going a mile."

"Joe, can she win the damn thing or not?" Charlie asked, his patience being tried to the very end.

"Lisa, call Amanda and get her over here. It's going to be a long night," Joe exclaimed.

As Lisa Marie made the call Joe looked over the horses that he would ride. The first for him would be the first race of the night, he was to ride a three year old gelding trained by Randy Watson. The gelding had raced five times prior to tomorrow nights race. He didn't show much promise.

The next one would be the second race, which was trained by Harvey Drake, the form had the gelding he would ride picked to run fourth, scanning over the past performances of his mount showed that the gelding didn't have a lot of speed. In his last four races he had been beaten a total of twenty two lengths. But something caught Joseph's eye. Before the last four races, his last race had been the previous year, as a two year old. Something had happened to him, but what? Joe concluded two things, either the horse wasn't fit which wasn't likely or the jock was scared of him. Joe went with the latter. The geldings name was Bobs Cowboy and was at the top of Joe's list.

"Dad, I think we might have a winner in the second," Joe told his father as he went on to the next race, which was the fifth.

After setting the telephone down Lisa Marie told father and son. "Amanda said she'd be here in about twenty minutes."

"Good, now let's work this out, we don't have much time before he calls back for an answer," Joe told them.

"Where do we start, Joseph?" Lisa Marie asked.

"I think I can win the second, but let's see what the rest looks like. In the fifth, I ride a horse called Time Out. He's picked to run…never mind."

"What's wrong with that one?" Charlie asked his son.

"I'll put it this way, Dad, he's named right."

"Okay, what's next?"

"The sixth I'm picked to run third, let's take a look and see. His name is Poker Aces, the race is a non-winners of three lifetime for seventy five-hundred. They're going a mile and a six tenth. He ran fifth his last out for ten-thousand, going three quarters. He was on the engine until the last seventy yards, when they ran past him. Looks like he's got one speed, what do you think, Dad, if I keep him on the lead the whole way."

"Let me see the form Joe," Charlie said, and then looking down at the charts of the sixth race. He then after careful consideration said, "Joe, if you do get the lead, you better get as far out in front as you can, and pray they don't gun you down."

""But can he maintain?" Joe asked.

"I just don't know, let's see what else you ride." He then handed the racing form back to his son.

After turning to the seventh race, Joe said, "Well, it's about time, I'm picked to win, this one. Damn it! Amanda rides this one!"

"What else does she ride, Joe?" Charlie asked.

"It looks like…we're screwed, she rides this one and the third, that's the only two she rides," Joe said, in heavily laden words.

Speaking up Lisa Marie added, "I'll bet the lunatic played it that way on purpose."

"Imagine that," Joe replied, and then started looking again.

"I've got a live one in the eighth, Dad."

"What's it look like Joe?" Charlie asked.

"It's going a flat mile, and the horse can go the distance, Dad, he likes to come from out of it, sometimes he gets a little late. But he's never out of the money. I can win this one," Joe told them with enthusiasm.

"So which two is it gonna be, Joseph?" His father asked.

"The one in the sixth looks good, and since Amanda has to win the seventh. I have to go with the one in the eighth, a horse by the name of, Shomethemoney."

A knock at the door brought a, "Who is it?" From Lisa Marie.

"It's Amanda," the voice from the other side said.

After looking through the peep hole in the door, Lisa Marie opened it with a, "Hello, Amanda, come on in."

"What's all this about, Joe?" Amanda asked.

"Well, for starters, have you ever won two races on a single card?" Answering her question with a question, Joe then waited for her answer.

"No, I can't say as I have," she replied.

"Well, tomorrow night you will, that's for sure."

"We've got some things to work out, don't we?" Amanda asked.

"We sure do, so you might as well pull up a chair and get comfortable."

Pulling up a chair beside Joe she said, "You know, I've got a pretty good shot of winning the third."

"Yeah, they have you picked to finish second. But we're going to see if we can get you moved up a couple of lengths. Now let's see, here we are the number four horse. Her name is, Ladysniteout, that's appropriate," Joe told them with a short smile. And then he asked, "So what do you know about her, Amanda?"

"Well, as you can see, I've ridden her six of the seven times she has ran, I broke her maiden, three starts back. That was in Houston, going a mile for ten thousand. Her last out at the same distance for seventy five hundred, I hate to admit it, but I got her beat."

Cutting her off, Joe asked. "How did you do that?"

"I was laying third as we started down the stretch, a hole opened on the fence, I waited just a hair then I started into it but it was to late. It closed up on me."

"Stop, I already know. You got boxed in, right," Joe said, interrupting her.

"Yeah, that about sums it up, when I could get to the outside, it was to late. I finished third. I should have won it, though."

"Well, it looks to me like the handicapper laid the odds and picks so that he could gamble," Charlie said, putting in his two cents.

"So what are you going to do different this time?" asked Joe.

"Well, I know that my filly's the best of the bunch, I'd say keep her out of trouble and let her run her own race."

"That sounds good, Amanda, you do know what the stakes are if you lose?" Lisa Marie asked the lady jock.

"Lisa, unfortunately I do," Amanda replied.

"Okay, have we got that settled?" Joe asked and, seeing everyone nod their heads, he continued. "Now the next one, Amanda, is going to be a little bit harder. It's the seventh race." After pausing long enough to turn the pages, he started again. "The worst of it is that I'm picked to win and, Amanda, you're a ten to one shot in the dark."

"How are we going to get this turned around Joe?" Amanda asked.

Replying, Joe said, "Well first of all, what do you know about your horse, Amanda, other than he's not to fast?"

"I've ridden him the last three times he's run, and he finishes with a kick, but it's not enough."

"I see that, Amanda, I also see he's been going a mile and an eighth, this time they have him backed up to a mile. Do you think that helps him or what?" Joseph asked.

"Depends, on how the race unfolds," she told him.

"That's where you're wrong, Amanda, good riders, with any kind of horse under them, they make it unfold the way they want it to. You might get out run, but you never get beat. Isn't that right, Dad?"

"That's right, Joseph, I taught you well," Charlie commented.

"So how do I apply it her, Joe?" Amanda asked.

"Just like this, I'm on a horse with speed. The other riders look for me to go to the front, back up the speed and kick hard down the lane. I'm willing to wager that while they think I'm backing it up, actually I'm going to set blazing fractions, while you get lost in the back. These boy's will be knocking on my back door, burning up gas, then when you hit the three eighths pole, I want you to go to work. You should run by 'em like they were tied to a pole."

"And how are you going to explain why you burnt your horse up on the lead?" Amanda asked.

Replying, Joe answered, "Little lady, that's how I've been making my living for the last twelve years."

While the foursome were going over the intricate details of their perspective races. There was another, going over notes, left behind by two deceased F.B.I. agents, Agent Conners and Agent Russo.

David Pearce had been with the F.B.I. going on eleven years, he considered himself street smart, and not to much got by him. However, this case got crazier and crazier damned near with each passing minute.

The crime lab report that he had, and was now going over, said that there was along with the traces of mud, there was also traces of horse manure, in Mrs. Gunn's room, where the Leblanc children had been abducted.

There was also the note pad that Conners had been keeping notes of the case on. Which really didn't show anything out of the normal, at least up until he had been killed. One thing that kept coming to his mind though, was how in the world did you get a boy of eleven, and a girl fifteen years old out of a house and no body see's or hear's anything. The more he thought about that, the more he became amazed.

There were so many blanks to fill in. He did know this through experience, that once the answers started coming, they would come like a landslide.

Back in the Leblanc's motel room, Amanda had just left. The Headless Horseman had called, the races had been chosen. Now Joe was saying. "You know Dad, as well as I do, that these people, want turn Mom and the kids loose no matter what we do."

"Joseph, I've been thinking pretty hard about that, somehow we're going to have to draw them out in the open. Don't ask me how, cause I don't hava clue of how to go about it."

As Charlie said these things to his son, Lisa Marie was just finishing up with the phone call to her mother.

"How was her flight?" Joe asked his wife.

"Non-eventful was her exact words. She wants to have breakfast though. She also want's a complete run down on what's going on with the Headless Horseman," Lisa told her husband.

"Did you tell her that nothing's changed, we aren't any closer now to getting them back than we were three day's ago?" Joseph asked.

"I believe she knows that, she just doesn't know what to say, Joseph."

"Hell, we're in the middle of it and don't know what to say, I can imagine how she feels," Joe said to his wife.

"Lisa, me and Joe were just talkin about the situation we're in. What we need to do is to start trackin' 'em instead of bein' run by 'em," Charlie said.

"Well, Dad, whada ya think we should do?" Joseph asked his dad while taking off his boots.

"For starters, let's start a list, of who could get so close as to know details of our lives."

Lisa Marie took out a piece of paper and a pencil. "Okay, where do we start?" she asked.

All three looked at each other, each hoping that someone would say something. Finally Charlie spoke up. "Well, let's put that, what's his name? That turkey, you ran into today."

"Billy Cox, Dad."

"We never did hear back from Pearce, did we?" Lisa said in a statement more than a question.

"No, we didn't, I say we put him at the top of the list," Charlie told his son and daughter- in-law.

Writing down his name on the paper in front of her, Lisa Marie asked, "Now what?"

Nobody had an answer for that one. Neither did anyone have an answer to that question a half hour later when the three called it a night.

Agent Pearce though was still on the job, going over notes, comparing Conners notes to the ones found in Russo's motel room. He was racking his brain trying to figure it out. Then he saw something Agent Conner's had jotted down, that he was waiting on a wire tap on Tracy Gunn's phone. He never received it though or at least he hadn't wrote it down before he had died. That was something he wanted to check on first thing in the morning. He doubted that it would lead to anything since Lisa Leblanc had left for Carrencro, the morning that the tap was to be placed, evidently he didn't know that her stay was going to be so short.

In Russo's notes there was the mention of Lisa's father and that he had been killed some years back and that his murder had never been solved. The local authorities in Beaumont, Texas had handled the case. That was something he also wanted to look into. Pearce had long been a gut player, and his gut was now telling him that this went a lot deeper than what the naked eye could see.

Meanwhile in the R.V., Maggie was herself going over some things in her mind.

What kept sticking in her thoughts though was what her grandchildren had said about Gerard's death, that it, in someway had something to do with what was going on now. But try as she might she couldn't imagine how. She was thinking back to the night, that he had been killed. Maggie's memory went to the conversation she had been having with Tracy that night in the Clubhouse of Vinton Downs. Tracy had been scared that Gerard was going to get hurt in a racing accident. That was the reason that she and little Lisa had come along with him. She said, she needed to be near him.

Why had Gerard gone to the store so late? When they had just come back from eating. What could have been so important that it couldn't wait until morning? Maggie didn't have any answers to these questions.

She brought herself back to the present with one single thought, she needed to figure out a way to escape or at least get the children out of here. She knew that their time was limited. Something had to be done and done quickly. But what, she had no idea.

The next morning found Pearce already on the phone with a detective from the Beaumont Police Department. The detectives name was Miller. He himself had not been old enough at the time of

Gerard Fontenot's death for it to have made any impression on him. However he had told Pearce that he would look into it. If nothing else he could find out who had handled the case, and that he would give Pearce a call back sometime after lunch.

Brian and Joe had left the motel, headed for the racetrack, way before the sun peaked over the horizon. They were now having coffee in the track cafeteria.

"Well, Joe, it looks like you and me make a pretty good team, wouldn't you say?"

"Not bad Brian, not bad at all," Joe told his agent while taking a sip of coffee.

Out of the corner of his eye he saw Billy Cox sitting at another table, smoking a cigarette, while talking to an older man.

Joe's thoughts went back to when he had run into Billy the morning before. Billy had told him in short that he had caused all of his bad luck and pretty much held Joe personally responsible. Joe had turned his head toward Billy and was now studying him and was thinking, is this man capable of killing two F.B.I. agents, and kidnaping his children.

"Hey, Joe," A female voice said, bringing him back from his thoughts.

Looking up, he saw Amanda holding a cup of coffee. "Good morning, Amanda, pull up a chair," he told the girl jockey. Then adding, after she had sat down, "This is my agent, Brian Gunn, Brian, meet Amanda Davis."

Offering his hand, he said, "Hello, Amanda, nice to meet you."

"Same here, Brian," she replied.

"Do you have an agent, Amanda?" Brian asked.

"Yeah, I do—Mike Hayes. He's had my book since Houston last year."

"Is he doing you any good?"

"Not really, but he's all I've got for now," she told Brian.

"You know pretty soon we're going to have a lot more business, than we can handle, maybe you might be looking for a change," Brian told her.

But what was going through Joe's mind was. "What in the hell is he doing."

"I don't think so, Mr. Gunn," she said, and then directed her next statement toward Joseph. "Joe, I've got to get busy, can we talk later?" she asked.

"Sure, where do you want to meet?"

Answering, she said, "back here, how's that sound?"

"Great."

After Amanda had walked away, Joe asked Brian. "What were you doing? Trying to pick up her book or what?"

"Yeah, you wouldn't mind, would you?" Brian asked.

"I don't know how I feel about that, but I'll let you know," Joe said to him.

Lisa Marie had just finished talking with Agent Pearce about Billy Cox.

In Pearce's opinion, Cox was not their man, sure he had been in trouble a couple of times, but for small stuff, nothing big.

After talking with Mrs. Leblanc, Pearce called the F.B.I. office in Bossier City, Louisiana and talked with Tim Jones. Tim and Pearce had known each other for about eight years and had helped one another on several occasions. Pearce had asked Tim if he would ask a few questions out at the track there about Brian Gunn.

Just maybe Russo was on to something with Gunn, and had only changed his mind after seeing his killer.

Lisa Marie after her conversation with Pearce she dialed up her mother's room. "Good morning, Mom," she said.

"Morning, Lisa, I see you're up and about," Tracy told her daughter.

"Yeah, I've been up since Joe left for the track."

"Me, too, honey. Are you ready for some breakfast and coffee yet?"

"We sure are, are you ready? They have a pretty decent café up front," Lisa told her.

"I'll be right over." After having said that, the call was ended.

Lisa and her mother along with Charlie had just ordered coffee as Lisa was saying, "So, Mom, how long are you planning on staying?"

"Oh, I don't really know for sure, for a week or so anyway." Pausing to add some cream to her coffee, she then directed her attention to Charlie. "You're looking good, Charlie. Are you holding up alright?"

Answering, Charlie said, "Thank you, Tracy, and yeah, I'm holding up okay, considering my wife and grandchildren are at the mercy of some damned lunatic."

"So do y'all have any idea at all who's really behind all of this?"

"No, Mom, we don't, seems like the minute, we have a lead it drops out from under us. As it is, he has us jumping through hoops like some animal in a circus."

The waitress had walked up at this point asking. "Are y'all ready to order, or should I come back?"

"No, no, I'm ready, little lady..." Charlie exclaimed.

Mean while at the R.V., their captor had brought the kids and their grandmother breakfast from the Tastee Freeze down the road.

Whispering to her grandson. "Now, Bradly when we get finished eating, just like yesterday, he's going to take you to the bathroom, when you step back, here, this is..." She had gone over this three times with him, but now the time was at hand, taking the step he moved to the side quickly, just as Maggie rose from the bed and with everything she had, just like kicking some old football, her foot connecting with his crotch, he let out a whoosh of air as he doubled over in agony as both Lanette and Maggie pounced on him.

"Run, Bradly, Run!!!" Maggie had screamed.

Bradly had taken flight as he raced for the front door of the R.V...he made it...unlocked it and was gone like a flash!

"You stupid bitch! What the hell!!" The man was screaming, as he crawled away from the two women. Finally he was able to climb to his feet, he then started for the door. He knew that he had screwed up bad.

Bradly didn't have any idea where he was at, nothing looked familiar, absolutely nothing. He just kept running and running down this dirt road. All the time wondering, where am I.

The man had made it outside, but he was hurt. Blood ran from his nose, and he was sure that he would have at least one black eye. However his biggest problem was the kid had gotten away. How in the world was he going to explain this? The thought of it was beginning to make him sick.

"Which way did he go?" he asked himself. "Damn it!" He said aloud.

Bradly saw a car coming his way. "Great!" He said as he began to run out of breath. And then he was waving his arms for the car to stop. Which it did, the man driving was by himself. He let the window down saying, "My lord, son, what in the world's the matter?"

"God, mister, am I glad to see you, my sister and grandma are being held in a big motor home right down the road here!" Bradly said as he tried to catch his breath.

"Whoa now, hold on there. What are you talkin about?"

"Me and my sister somebody kidnaped us, come on mister, we have to go call the police! Hurry please!"

"Come on now, son, get in the car! I've got a cell phone that we can call the police on."

Getting in the car Bradly asked. "Where are we anyway?"

"Why Bradly, you're in Texas, San Antone to be exact," the man said as he grinned.

Something was wrong, very wrong. "How do you know my name?" Bradly asked the man, he knew though that he had made a mistake by getting in the car with this man. Bradly made a decision at that very moment...

Over at the racetrack, Joe had just finished breezing a three year old filly for Johnny Wade. He was now headed for the racing office to find his agent. He wanted to know what Brian had lined up for him after the break.

Charlie and Lisa Marie had walked Tracy back to her motel room. They themselves had driven over to Texas Downs. They were hoping to catch Joseph during the break. Looking first in the track cafeteria, not having any luck they then walked over to the racing office.

As Joe was walking out, they were walking in. "Hey, you two," Joe said, greeting them.

"We were just looking for you," Lisa Marie said to her husband.

"Well, I was looking for Brian, have y'all seen him anywhere?"

"No we haven't, but I'll bet he shows up in the cafeteria," Lisa said.

"Well, let's go see, besides I need something cold to drink. I hope I don't have very many to get on after the break," Joe told his wife and father as they walked toward the air-conditioned café.

Bradly upon getting into the man's car had noticed the large Styrofoam cup filled with steaming liquid. The man was holding it in one hand and driving with the other. At the first sign of foul play, Bradly had hit the man's arm and hand that held the cup, spilling the hot liquid in the man's lap and stomach. The man had screamed and then slamming the car in park trying to get away from the liquid that was now burning the hell out of him. He had for an instant forgot about Bradly, and that's exactly when Bradly made his next move which was exiting the car as quickly as he could. He was now running through some woods as fast as his feet would carry him. He had no idea where he was running to. He only knew that he was somewhere in Texas, and that there were bad people everywhere.

The man in the car had chased Bradly for about a hundred yards before he gave up. He was no match for an eleven year old that was for sure. Getting back to his car, he was met by his partner in crime. "Did you see the boy?" the man from the R.V. asked.

"No asshole, I was chasin' a rabbit, out through the woods! What I want to know is, how in the world did you let him get away in the first place, and next, I'd also like to know how you let an old woman and two kids beat the hell out of you? Never mind, I really don't give a shit one way or the other," The man told his partner these things as he climbed back into his car. "Well, are you gonna get in or what?" he asked.

The man from the R.V. got into the car, they then drove the short distance to the prison on wheels.

"Look, I want you to check on them, make sure that they're secure, then I want you to get out there and find that kid. Do you understand me?"

"Yeah, I got it, I'll find him."

"You damn well better!"

Both men got out of the car, the R.V. man stepped into the camper, seeing the two women he turned and said, "Everything is good in here."

"Great, now get busy, findin' that damn kid," the man replied and then got back in his car. "I'll be back later to check on you," he said through his opened window. He then backed out and was gone.

Inside the R.V., Maggie was saying, "Sh,sh now, Lanette, I know that voice, but I don't know where from, why is it so familiar?"

"I don't know grandmom, I just hope Bradly's alright?" Lanette said.

"Baby, I think Bradly's gonna be just fine. Did you see how brave he was and fast, like lightnin?" Maggie said, proudly of her grandson.

In the meantime F.B.I. special Agent Pearce was catching hell from his boss. "You mean to tell me Pearce, that I've got two dead agents, and the jockey that's in the middle of all of this, is still riding in races! Not to mention the three that have been kidnaped, and you don't have not one goddamned clue as to who this goddamned Headless Horseman asshole is? Is that what you're telling me?"

David Pearce was glad for one thing and one thing only, and that was the fact that he was not with his boss in person, but on the telephone. "Sir, no we don't really have a sus..." Pearce was cut short.

"Pearce, listen to what I say, you better have a hell of a lot more when I call you tomorrow, than what you have right now! Are we clear on that?"

"Yes, sir, crystal clear." His boss had ended the call. Jesus H. Christ, Pearce thought, what in the hell else can happen?

Pearce, after regrouping, dialed up the Bossier City office of his friend, Tim Jones. After the third ring, it was answered. "Jones, here," the voice on the line said.

"Yeah, Tim, it's me, Pearce."

"Hey, Dave, I was just going to call you."

"Some good news I hope," Pearce told his friend.

"Well, I really don't know what kind of news it is. I asked around about the guy, and sure they knew him but they acted pretty much like they haven't seen him in awhile."

"Really, I was under the impression that he just left there."

"David, I don't know what to tell ya, I ran a back ground check on the man, he came up clean. I really don't think he fits the profile."

"Yeah, you're probably right. Well hey, thanks for tryin', I really appreciate it"

"No problem old pal, I gotta go. Stay in touch."

After hanging up the phone Pearce just sat there in his room closing his eyes for just a moment and thinking, this is really starting to stink bad. Okay, so Brian Gunn doesn't fit the profile, then who in the hell does?

At the track Joe and Brian were talking about the mounts Brian had picked up for Joe to ride the next evening. All together out of a ten race card, Joe had been named on nine horses that would go to the post and race.

"Joe, you have caught on here like wild fire, this is great!" Brian said.

"Brian, let's not forget why I'm really here, it's not about winning races, it's about getting my mother and my kids back."

"Of course it is, Joe. It just feels good to be winning races. Do you realize I haven't had a hot rider like this in a very long time.

"I'm glad for you, and lord knows I needed your help, but I'm giving it some serious thought that when this whole thing is over, I might just give up riding races altogether."

"You can't be serious," Brian said in disbelief.

"You know, Brian, I have always wanted to be a jockey, ever since I was just a kid. Well, I became one, and a damned good one at that, but look at what it has cost me. It has cost me everything that I have ever held dear to my heart. Do you think that if I would have stayed in Carrencro, and went to work in the oilfield I'd be having these problems right now?"

"Joe, I doubt it very much so," Brian said. Then after a short pause, as if he were collecting his thoughts he added, "Enough, about this for now, I gotta get to the racing office. I'll catch up with you later. Okay?"

"Sounds good, Brian, and Brian, I don't think that I told you, but I am now—thank you for helping us."

"Joseph, it's been my pleasure."

Joe was now on his way back to the track cafeteria to meet back up with his wife and dad, also Amanda had said earlier that she wanted to talk about something, what, he didn't know...

After sitting down at the table with Lisa and Charlie, he had finished off about half of his grapefruit juice when Amanda walked in. "Over here, Amanda," Joe said while motioning her over to their table.

"Hi, Lisa, Mr. Leblanc. I didn't know if you might have forgotten that I needed to talk to you."

"No, Amanda, I didn't forget, whats on your mind?" Joe asked.

"Joe, I've been riding now for about five years, even though I didn't win a lot of races, I was at least confidant that while doing something that I love doing, I could make a living doing it."

Pausing for just a second as to choose her words carefully. Joseph cut in asking. "What are you tryin' to say, Amanda?"

"It's just that...why did these people choose me to team up with you? You wanta know what I did last night after I left yalls room...I'll tell you, what I did. I went home and got on my computer and looked up Mr. Joseph Leblanc through the archives of jockey's and their records. Somewhere along the way, somebody forgot to inform me just who you were."

Cutting in again, Joe asked, "What in the hell are you talkin' about, Amanda?"

"I'm talking about an eclipse winner, a leading apprentice in the nation, a Derby winner, and so on and so on winding up to date, a grand slam total of five thousand and twenty one victories. Joe Leblanc, nobody else might not be intimidated but I sure as hell am." Nobody said a word for at least a good thirty seconds. Finally Joe, was the first to speak. "Well, tonight, just think, the whole racing world is going to see Amanda Davis, female jock extraordinaire undress the great and infamous Joseph Leblanc, down the stretch in the seventh race." Everyone at the table smiled, with Amanda shaking her head as she added, "Well, I'll be damned."

Joe then continued, "I want you to know, Amanda, that whatever I'm doing now, whether it be not letting a horse win or clocking so that you can win is, by no means the ethical thing to do. I did it for a long time because I was afraid that someone in my family would get hurt if I didn't play the game. It doesn't make it right. And, Amanda, this is sure not a game without consequences, before it's over, we'll all know exactly what hell is like. I wish it weren't true, but it is.

It's RACING!

Bradly could see the man through the trees, but he was sure the man couldn't see him. He was tucked down in a ravine with brush and branches hiding him, he had barely been small enough to fit. He was now almost holding his breath as the man drew near. Uh oh, he thought, the man had stopped. He seemed to be looking right at Bradly, was he?...No, he was looking past Bradly and then he heard the man curse. "Damn it all to hell, that damn kid of Leblanc's! Screw it, this will all be over soon anyway."

Bradly sat very still, he kept his eyes trained on the man, and then he turned and walked in the direction from where he had come. Bradly still didn't move, however he was hot and very thirsty as the Texas sun beat down upon him.

Pearce was still in his motel room when his cell phone beckoned him to answer. "Hello, Pearce here."

"Pearce, this is detective Miller, I've got some information for you on the Fontenot case."

"That's great detective, what have you got?"

"The detective, that worked the case retired two years ago. Turns out he's actually a friend of my dad's. I gave him a call to see if he might want to talk about it, he does, says there were some things that bothered him about the case and the way it went down. At any rate, here's his number,…names Ron McGuire, and Pearce, good luck to ya."

"Thanks a million," Agent Pearce told the detective and then he ended the call. After that he dialed Mr. McGuire's number, after the fourth ring it was answered. "Hello," the voice said, on the other end of the line.

"Yes sir, could I speak with a Mr. Ron McGuire please?"

"Speaking, what can I do for ya?"

"Mr. McGuire, my names David Pearce and I'm with the F.B.I."

Cutting the agent short he said, "Oh, yeah, I've been expecting your call, Mr. Pearce. How can I help you?"

"Well, for starters, you can call me David."

"Okay, David, since we're dropping the formalities, please call me Ron."

Having worked that out Pearce started again. "Ron, detective Miller told me that you worked on the Fontenot murder case back in the early 70s."

"Sure did. Never did solve the damn thing, though. I had some ideas, but the upper brass argued that it was just a plain old robbery. I never did buy into it, to many thing's just didn't add up…" The retired detective told these thing's to agent Pearce as he himself drifted back in time.

"Ron, there must have been something that really stuck out for you to remember this case like you have."

"There were a couple of things that did. For starters, if it was just a robbery, why did he still have his wallet in his back pocket. Now, I ain't never robbed anyone but if I were to, you can bet on this for sure. If I go to all the trouble of goin all the way out in the country, and shoot'en your ass, believe me I'm goin to go through your wallet, and I'm damn sure not gonna put it back where I found it. Are we on the same page, Dave?"

"Yes, sir, I believe we are at that," Agent Pearce replied.

"Another thing that had me puzzled was the fact that the clerk, at the store where Fontenot stopped, had stated that Fontenot had bought a pack of Marlboros and a Dr. Pepper..." McGuire was letting that set in before he continued, "Now, Dave, if an ol country dog like myself can figure this out, I'm sure that a special agent from the F.B.I. will have no problem with it..."

"Mr. McGuire, I don't mean any disrespect but I've got a lot on my plate and times wastin'..."

"Oh alright, the facts are this, Fontenot wasn't a smoker nor was his wife and no cigarette butts in his ashtray,

nor was there any Dr. Pepper bottle in his car, are you understanding what I just said?"

"Who was he buying the cigs for? He knew the killer! didn't he?"

"Well, I'll be damned, even the F.B.I. can figure that out, but the brass I worked for said, that it didn't have any bearing. What the real deal was, is that they didn't give a damn about some jockey from Louisiana, coming over here and get'n his ass killed."

"Tell me something, Ron, did you personally have any suspects that you were looking at?" Pearce asked.

"Well, not really, but anytime that you assume foul play, you go for the people nearest to the victim," McGuire offered.

"Yeah, like family, or maybe Fontenot was having an affair," Pearce said.

"That's always a possibility, the strange thing though is that Fontenot had not been around this part of the country for a number of years," Ron McGuire told the agent.

"So all we really know is this, Fontenot was buying cigarettes for somebody just before he was killed," Pearce stated, then added, "Is it safe to assume that the killer smokes Marlboro's or at least that he was with someone else?"

"I'd say so, Pearce. But who you might want to talk with is the clerk at the store, if he's still alive or around. Just a minute and I'll get you his name, I kept a personal file of my own."

Pearce was thinking that the Fontenot case must have really ate on him pretty good to have kept a personal file on it.

"Pearce, you still there?" McGuire asked.

"Sure am," he answered.

"The guy's name is Ed Spencer, the last phone number that I had was…, you gotta pen and paper?" he asked.

"Yeah, go ahead."

"It's…got it?"

"Sure do, Mr. McGuire. I want to thank you for your help."

"Not a problem. If I can do anything else for you, let me know."

After the two had ended the call Pearce dialed the number given to him by McGuire. After the sixth ring Pearce was just about to hang up when a gruffy voice said, "Hello"

"Yes sir, is this Ed Spencer?" Pearce asked.

"Yeah, this is him, who's this?"

"Mr. Spencer, my name is David Pearce and I'm with the F.B.I…hello, hello! That son of a gun hung up on me!" Not being intimidated, Pearce dialed up the number again, this time after the second ring it was answered by a machine. "Hello, we're not home at this time, however if you'll leave a message and your number we'll get back in touch with you."

Pearce knew that Spencer wasn't away, so he didn't leave a message, he did however say this, "Mr. Spencer, this is Agent Pearce, at this time, you're not under arrest. Hell, as far as I'm concerned you haven't broken any laws. Unless you answer this phone you will be in more trouble…"

"Hello, hey! This is Ed Spencer."

"Very good, Mr. Spencer, you made a good decision. The reason I'm calling you is that I need some information about the Fontenot murder."

"You mean that jockey who got killed? Man, that was a long time ago!"

"Yeah, you're right, Mr. Spencer, it was a long time ago. But I still need to ask you some questions."

"Look, man, I told the cops everything I knew way back when it happened. I don't think I could tell you anything else that would help."

"Maybe not, but I still have some questions for you." Pearce didn't know why his gut was telling him to push and pump this guy, but his gut wasn't wrong very often, so he pressed on. "For starters, how did the police know that Fontenot had stopped in the store, where you worked?"

"I really don't know, as a matter of fact, I really never thought about it. But they did. You see, I had just started my shift, I was working twelve hour shifts back then which meant that I worked from twelve midnight till twelve noon." Spencer, had paused for a moment as if he were collecting his thoughts.

Pearce would not interrupt the man, for he was opening up. There were answers here, he could feel it.

"Mr. Pearce, I was young back then, and I sure wasn't lookin for any trouble, nor am I lookin for any now. But I think that there was a lot more to that jockey gettin killed than what meets the eye, know what I mean?"

Joseph, his dad, and Lisa Marie were contemplating their next move.

"So, Dad, what do you think we should do?" Joe asked his father.

"Damned if I know. Maybe we should start lookin a little closer at Mr. Billy Cox," Charlie said.

"You might be right, Dad, but how do we go about it?"

"Well, speak of the devil. Look who just walked in," Lisa Marie said.

Billy Cox was now in line for some coffee, he was not aware of the three sets of eyes that bore down on his back.

"Maybe we should follow him, that might get us some answers. What do you think?" Said, Joseph.

"I'd say I'm a lot more for it, than I am against it," Charlie said.

"Well, let's go on out to the pickup, we can see him when he comes through the gate," Lisa Marie told the two men. And with that the three got up and walked outside.

"Grandmom, do you think Bradly's okay?" Lanette asked.

"Oh, I'm sure he'll be just fine," Maggie told her granddaughter. But inside she wasn't so sure. He'd been gone now for what seemed like an eternity, although it probably hadn't been but just an hour or so.

"We don't even know where we're at, we drove a long way; didn't we?" Lanette said.

"I'm afraid so baby. But try not to worry. I know it's hard. What we need to be doin' is prayin." Maggie was trying not to show just how scared she was. She hoped that it was working.

In the meantime, Bradly had come out of his hiding place, however he had no idea in which direction to go. He knew that he didn't want to go back in the direction from which he had come. He reasoned though that if he waited until dark he'd be able to see some lights, which would give him a sense of directions. Instead of heading off out into the desert. So he crawled back into his cubby hole to wait and to say a prayer for his sister and grandmother.

Joe, his wife, and Charlie were following Billy Cox about four cars back. They were on interstate ten headed east.

"Where do you think he's goin?" Joe asked as he switched over into the left hand lane to pass an old chevy pickup.

"I have no idea, Joseph," Lisa Marie said to her husband.

His father said nothing as if to say, "That doesn't warrant an answer."

"We've come about thirty miles,…wait, look, he's gettin' off at the rest area," Lisa Marie said.

"Dad, what should I do?" Joseph asked.

"Don't get off Joe, we'll go to the next exit. He has to come that way, even if he doesn't exit off the interstate, we'll see him go by," Charlie told his son.

F.B.I. Agent David Pearce, was now sitting in his motel room, and trying to figure out how the information he had obtained was going to help him solve this case. Mr. Spencer had told him something that he had not told the detectives all those years ago. It wasn't just going to help Pearce solve the case he was now working on but also the murder of Gerard Fontenot. First though, he would need to confirm a few things, which wasn't going to be easy. These were his thoughts as he picked up his phone. He punched in a number and then waited for the answer. One ring, two, then three. "Hello," a voice on the other end said.

While Agent Pearce was making his phone calls, there were three Leblancs waiting at a filling station watching cars go by. "Damn, Dad, what in the world could he be doing all this time?" Joseph asked his father.

"Damned if I know," Charlie replied, then, looking at his watch, added. "We've been sittin' here for more than an hour."

"Whadaya think we should do?" Joe asked.

"We better head back toward San Antone," Lisa Marie told her husband.

"Yeah, I'd say so, too, Lisa. I'm gonna have to be in the jock's room before long."

"I'd have to agree," Charlie added.

As they past the rest area on the way back, looking on the opposite side of the interstate Lisa Marie spotted Billy Cox's vehicle. "Look, there's Billy's car."

"You know what kids, I think Billy pulled a fast one on us," Charlie said.

"How so Charlie?" Lisa asked.

Cutting in Joseph said, "You think he got into another car?"

"I'd say that's exactly what he did. But now we know he has something to hide, why else would he leave his car and take another?" Charlie said.

"Do you think that we can assume all of that?" Lisa asked.

"It's all we have to go on so far. You know what Joe, I think that after we drop you off at the track, I'm coming back out here and wait for Mr. Billy Cox," Charlie told his son.

"Oh no, not by yourself, no way!" Joe protested.

"I'm not going to confront him Joseph, I just want to find out for myself what in the hell the little bastards up to."

"Dad, I wish you wouldn't do that, and I sure as hell, don't want Lisa out here either."

"I'm stayin' at the grandstand to watch these races," Lisa Marie told them.

"Well, why don't I get Brian to come with me, that way Tracy can stay with you, Lisa," Charlie said.

"I'd have to admit we need to keep an eye on Billy," Joe told his father.

"Then it's settled Joe, providing Brian will do it," Charlie said.

Then the three Leblanc's seemed to drift off into their own thoughts as they barrelled back to San Antone.

Agent Pearce had made the phone calls that he needed to make. Now he was sitting back and waiting for the calls to come back in. Which shouldn't be very much longer, of course that would be just the first step to exposing the Headless Horseman, and possibly solving a murder that had taken place over twenty years ago.

Back at the R.V., Lanette and her grandmother were trying to keep up their spirits. "Lanette, I know it doesn't look good, Bradly should have gotten to some help by now."

"You don't think they caught him. do ya?" Lanette asked.

"Baby. I just don't know, I wish I did," Maggie told her granddaughter, and then after taking a breath she added. "Come mornin, Lanette, if we haven't heard anything about your brother, well I got a little trick for our friend."

"What are you going to do?" she asked her grandmother.

"Don't you worry, we'll talk about it later." Maggie didn't have any idea of what she was going to do. But she could tell that Lanette needed some kind of hope. And besides, she had a feeling that come morning all hell was going to break loose.

Joe had been dropped off at the racetrack, and was now talking with Amanda as they waited for the races to begin.

"Are you ready for this, Amanda?" Joe asked.

"As ready as I'll ever be," Amanda replied.

The riders were now being called to the saddling paddock for the first race.

"Well, Amanda, I guess it's time to start the night, we want have much time to talk between races. I want you to know that I am really grateful for your help."

"Are you kiddin' me? How often does a female rider in south Texas get lessons in riding from the great Joe Leblanc?" Amanda smiled in such a way that Joe knew she was trying to lighten the moment, while also trying to let him know that she knew exactly, just how serious it was.

"Thanks, Amanda," is what Joe told her as he took his whip from his valet, and headed for the horses that were now saddled and waiting for their jockeys.

Meanwhile, Charlie and Brian had gone back to the rest area where Billy Cox's car sat. The two men were now sipping coffee from Styrofoam cups, they had purchased at the last exit.

"Brian, I want to thank you for coming out here with me tonight," Charlie said.

"Hell, Charlie, I'm glad I can help. I know that you and Gerard were pretty tight. I never meant to take his place."

"Brian, it's alright, that all happened a long time ago."

"Well, I'm glad you feel that way. I know this has been real hard on you."

"You're not wrong there, I feel like I've aged twenty years over the last few days."

"I'm sure, I can't even imagine what you're goin' through."

After having said that, the two sat there watching Billy's car as the night overcame the day.

At Texas Downs, in the grandstand, Lisa Marie and her mother had just watched the running of the first race.

The horse that her husband had ridden finished a bad third. Lisa Marie was silently thanking God, for Joseph not picking this one to win.

In the second race of the night Joe was in front until the eighth pole and then three ran past, with him finishing where he had been picked, fourth.

"Lisa Marie, I'm glad we've got this time together. I just hope everything turns out alright. Surely it will."

"Oh, Mom, I don't know what I'll do if this get's worse. I'm at my wits end."

"It's gonna be okay," Tracy told her daughter.

The track announcers voice came over the loud speaker.

"The horses are coming on to the track for the running of the third race, and will go to the post in less than twelve minutes, please place your wagers early."

Amanda looked at the tote board, as the procession of horses paraded by. Her horse, the number four was at six to one, she was the third choice of gamblers. However, as she told the pony girl. "Okay, Jan, let's go ahead and warm the big girl up." She felt very confidant in what she had to do.

In the jocks room, Joe was glued to the television monitor that would show the race. He was hoping that Amanda was not a bundle of nerves as he was.

In the grandstand, Lisa was telling her mother. "Mom, if this girl loses this race, I just don't know what I'll do."

"You'll keep going on, that's what you'll do. Sometimes the air just get's sucked out of you. Kind of like what happened to me when your father got killed."

"The horses are moving into the starting gate." The announcer stated, "Having a little trouble with Ladysniteout, whoa! Ladysniteout has just unseated her rider, Amanda Davis."

At that moment, the cell phone that Lisa Marie had in her purse began ringing. "Oh shit," Lisa said as she fumbled with it while her eyes stayed glued to the video screen...

"Hello," she answered.

"My-my, we sound a tad nervous," the voice said, and then after a short pause, as to deliver just the right amount of pressure, the voice continued. "In our agreement, the girl must win two races, there are no scratches, as a matter of fact, there will be no excuses, either she wins or she doesn't!" That was all he had said.

"Was that him?" Tracy asked her daughter.

"Yeah, Mom, it was," Lisa Marie answered, "Look, Mom, Amanda's back on!"

"Amanda Davis has regained her seat, as the assistants attempt to load her...there she goes! They're all in line and they'er racing...thats Ladysniteout, in front as they head into the club house turn, in second, two lengths back that's April Wine, another length back running third is Diamond Lucy." The track announcer, taking a short pause as to catch his breath, then continued, "They went the first quarter in twenty four flat, that's Ladysniteout, with Amanda Davis, still on the engine, with April Wine, right there in second."

In the jock's room, Joe was saying under his breath. "That's it, Amanda, you're doing great."

The announcer continued. "They've gone the half in forty eight and two, its still Laysniteout, in front, Diamond Lucy, is moving up to challenge April Wine, as they head into the far turn, here comes Bethsturn, up on the outside, but it's still all Ladysniteout, with Diamond Lucy, right there, April Wine, has sifted back to fourth as Bethsturn, has moved into third, as they turn for home. Diamond Lucy, moves up to challenge the leader, but Ladysniteout, will have none of it! As she easily puts Diamond Lucy away by opening a four and a half length lead over the field, they're at the wire with Ladysniteout, clearly the winner this evening."

In the jock's room, Joe finally took a breath. Jesus, he thought, what a race. "Amanda, you rode a great race. And thank you, God, for being with her."

In the grandstand, Lisa Marie showed no emotion as she too, told God, thank you. Her mother Tracy, didn't show emotion other than a smile, and before she could say anything the infamous cell phone beckoned once again to be answered. Lisa Marie answered. "Yeah!"

"We've dropped the formalities of hello, have we?" Not waiting for the reply on that, he continued. "Very well, now that's one down. Three to go." The line went dead.

"What did they say, Lisa?" her mother asked.

"Just telling me the score."

"That's all…that's it?" her mother inquired again.

"Pretty much, Mom. What else is there to say?" Lisa Marie answered in a curt sort of way.

"Lisa Marie, you don't have to take that tone with me, I was…"

Lisa, cutting her mother short, said, "I'm sorry, Mom, I didn't mean anything by it."

"Oh, it's okay, baby, I know you're under a lot of strain," Tracy told her daughter and then, putting her arms around her, said, "It's soon going to be over honey, you'll see. Everything is going to be okay."

Bradly was just crawling out of his hiding place. He had thought that the sun would never go down. He was so thirsty he could hardly swallow, and he was hungry. Looking in all directions most of the lights he saw came from where he had run from, however more to the right there seemed like a lot of lights all together, kind of like the lights at a softball field, or a "race track." And so that's the direction he decided on. As he started off he thought what I should do is go check on my sister and grandma. They must surely think something bad has happened to him. He wasn't sure what to do, but he didn't think it a bad idea to skirt the big R.V., besides it was dark.

Back at the track Joe had just been legged up on his horse, that he would ride in the fifth race. He didn't think that he had a very good chance at winning it, but you never know when a horse might fire a good race. As it's said, "Every dog has his day."

In the grandstand, Lisa Marie and her mother were watching the post parade. "There's Joe, Mom, he's the five horse."

"Look at the odds on him, Lisa."

"Yeah, thirty to one, doesn't look like he's got a chinaman's chance in hell," Lisa said.

"Well, it's a good thing that he doesn't have to win this one," Tracy told her daughter.

"You can say that again mother," Lisa replied.

Mean while, Bradly had come to the place where he thought the RV had been, as a matter of fact he was sure that it had been right here, but it wasn't. He could even feel the tracks that the tires had made!

Bradly was sick, he couldn't believe this was happening. The only thing he knew to do, was to keep moving toward the lights.

Back at the track, the fifth race had just ran, Joe's horse had finished way back, beating only one horse. And as he pulled his mount up short he was wondering, why had Brian, picked this horse up to ride, all it did was hurt his percentages. The next race however was a totally different ball game. He would win the sixth. There was no doubt!

While all of this was taking place F.B.I. Agent David Pearce had received confirmation on two of the three calls he had made. One more and he would have this in the bag. It would take a little doing and finesse, would be a must. But at least he had some direction. Which was a big change for this case.

The jock's room, twenty three minutes till post-time for the running of the sixth race at Texas Downs, found Joe Leblanc and Amanda Davis having a short conversation before he was due in the paddock.

"We want have a chance after this, Amanda, matter of fact, I'm really not comfortable talking with you now. I don't want anybody to suspect us of what we're about to do in the next race. Just stay to the plan," Joe said as he adjusted his helmet and responded to the call of the jockey's. "Good luck, Joe," Amanda offered.

Joseph only gave his quick smile as he went toward the paddock. Walking into the ring where the horses were now being saddled, Joseph looked out at the patrons and quickly saw his wife as she gave the good luck nod she had been giving him since the very first race he had ridden in.

"Hello, Joe, how ya doin' tonight?" the trainer of the horse he was to ride said.

"Pretty good, Tom, ready to win one. I know that."

"Well, that makes it unanimous, all you gotta do now is get it done, can you do it?"

"Yes, I will win this race Tom, bet the farm!" Joe said, with an iron will.

"Riders up!" the track official called.

Legging Joe on to the horse, Tom, the trainer said, "Good luck, Leblanc."

And then Joe and his mount Poker Aces were led out to the track, where the pony people would take the race horses from the grooms.

Joe had gone past where his wife stood, she had mouthed. "I love you!" He had done the same.

Riding races for Joe, was like breathing is to other people. It was just that simple. He never got rattled, and it didn't matter the circumstances. But this was different. The stakes were way to high. For the first time in his life Joe Leblanc, was as nervous as a whore in Sunday school.

"Hello there, Joe," Kim, the pony girl said as she took Poker Aces from the groom.

"How ya doin'?" Joe replied, he hadn't been there long enough to pick up their names yet. They had the advantage of looking up the jock's name in the program. Sometimes, Joe felt that the attention of the patron should cover the people behind the scenes, that made it possible for riders to win races.

"Let's go ahead and warm up a little," Joe said to Kim.

"You're the boss," the pony girl told him.

Going past the tote board, Joe had told himself earlier that he wouldn't look, he lied, he couldn't help it. Poker Aces, was a whopping fifteen to one. Jesus, I knew I should've looked, he told himself. Remember Joseph, horses can't read tote boards, and Jockey's shouldn't. That's what his dad, had always told him. Now if ever, he needed to apply that principle. Poker Aces was warming up good, he thought as they trotted in an oval circle. "That'll do it," he told Kim.

"Looks like he feels pretty good," she commented.

"Yeah, he's alright. I think he'll run good," Joseph said back to her. His mind was now mentally building the race and how it will unfold, he needed to get out in front to build the colts heart. Some horses are like that, if they didn't make the lead early they'd fizzle out. On the other hand, if they did make the lead sometimes their heart wouldn't give it up. That's what Joe was hoping for.

They were now headed for the starting gate. Poker Aces, had drawn the two hole, which meant that they would have to wait about a minute or so, maybe two depending how well they loaded.

They were now behind the gate and starting to load. The race was a mile and a sixteenth long. Which meant they would break from in front of the grandstand.

"Good luck, Joe," Kim told him.

"Thanks," Joe told her as he pulled down his goggles. The assistant starter had taken hold of Poker Aces and had started toward the number two slot. "Stay with me, partner," Joe told the handler.

"The two, need's headed, boss!" The assistant said to the starter.

"Stay then, Mike," the starter replied.

"Thanks, I need to be on the engine, ship me away from here, I owe you a hundred," Joe said.

"I got'cha, jock, they're one back, tie on," he told Joe.

There in the grandstand, but in front of the gate, Lisa Marie and her mother waited for the break.

They're all in line...and they're racing! Stumbling badly at the start, that's Poker Aces...

"God damn it!!!!" Joe said, while trying to keep his horse on his feet, after about two jumps, he managed to get Poker Aces back in the game, but there was no way to make the lead now. He had only an instant to make a split second decision...

"Damn it all to hell!!!" Lisa Marie screamed, as she ran back inside to watch the race on the monitor where she could get a better look at what was happening. The announcer was well into the call of the race. "As they enter the clubhouse turn, well bunched, that's Make a Wish in front, with Roman Randi, right there in second, a length back and to the inside is Gatlin Road, in third...

Joe had opted to not rush Poker Aces to the pack, he had blown his chance at the lead, and he knew it would use his horse up if he pushed it. So he just let the colt run on a loose rein.

"What in the hell is he doing?" Tracy asked her daughter.

"Don't worry, I have faith, Joe knows what he's doing."

"It's a damn wonder he even stayed on the horse," Lisa Marie said, defending her husband.

The track announcer in full swing and hoping for a dramatic finish. "Racing down the back side, that's still "Make a Wish" in front by a length and a quarter, followed up by "Roman Randi" in second, "Gatlin Road" right there also, up on the outside is "Prior Lake" in fourth, followed by "Texas Pride…""

"You can't even see him, he's so far behind," Tracy said.

"Quit it, Mom!" Lisa Marie said aloud, and then silently she said a prayer in her heart, "Please, God, don't let this happen."

""Roman Randi" has moved up along side "Make a Wish." Back a half length that's "Prior Lake" to the outside, with "Texas Pride" tucked in on the rail in fourth, then back another two lengths is "Booger Red…""

Charlie and Brian were still watching Billy Cox's car with no luck. However, they had tuned in to a radio station that gave the call of each race. Which they were now listening to the sixth race. "Damn it, this is the one where Joe needed to be on the front end," Charlie said.

"He hasn't even got a call yet, other than his horse stumbled, leaving the starting gate," Brian told Charlie.

"No, Brian, he got a call…that he was trailing the field."

The track announcer was winding everything up for his stretch call. "They're well into the far turn, it's still "Make a Wish" in front by a head, "Roman Randi" right there to challenge, "Prior Lake" making a move, so is "Texas Pride"…As they turn for home "Roman Randi" has taken the lead, while "Make a Wish" has started to fade. But for all he's worth here comes "Poker Aces"!!!!!! With less than an eighth of a mile to go "Roman Randi" still leads, "Texas Pride" is right there. "Poker Aces" right beside the leader…It's still "Roman

Randi" with "Poker Aces" right beside. They're nose for nose, head to head, it looks like a

battle, it's not a battle, it's a war!!! They're at the wire…it'll be a photo finish!"

Joseph's heart was pounding, he knew it was close, but he didn't know if he actually had won it.

"Jesus H. Christ!" Lisa Marie exclaimed. "Did he win it, Mom?"

"I don't know, Lisa, it was too close," Tracy said to her daughter.

The track announcer's voice came over the P.A. system.

"Ladies and Gentleman, please hold all tickets. While the stewards review the photo finish."

It took a little more than five minutes for the steward's to decipher who the winner was. Then finally, the track announcer, called the race official, "Ladies and gentleman, may I have your attention, after reviewing the photo finish the stewards had declared the number two, Poker Aces the official winner."

The weight of the world had just been lifted from the shoulders of Joseph Leblanc, or so it seemed, as he was led into the winners circle for the customary win picture to be taken.

Charlie Leblanc was telling Brian. "Lord, that boy was on the move, he came from dead-last to win!"

"Joe can surely ride when he has the right kind of incentive, wouldn't you say, Charlie?"

"Yes, he can, there's no tellin just how far he'd have gone if this Headless Horseman ass-hole, hadn't started jackin with him."

"Charlie, I think this might be a bust, evidently this Billy guy isn't coming back. At least not tonight," Brian said.

"Yeah, I guess you're right, you ready to head back?"

"Yes, I am," Brian answered. With that said, they started the return trip to San Antone.

Back at the race track and in the jock's room, Joe was hustling to get his silks changed.

Amanda, was already waiting for the call of the jock's to the paddock for the seventh race, when Joe came up behind her. "You ready for this?" he asked her.

Amanda simply answered, "Yes, I am, I'm ready."

"Let's go riders, to the paddock!" The clerk of scales, announced.

Joseph and Amanda said not a word, they knew what had to be done, and they were about to do it.

Joe's horse "Bobstoy" had drawn the six hole, and was now walking around the ring being led by his groom.

Amanda's mount for the seventh race was named "I'ma Jet," he had drawn the four hole.

The race itself was going one mile, which meant that they would start the race at the finish line.

"Bobstoy was trained by Robert Jenson, Joe didn't know the man. He did know that Mr. Jenson, figured he had a winner.

"How ya doin', Joe, I'm Bob Jenson. I figured it would be a good idea if I put you on a winner the first time we teamed up," the trainer said as he pumped Joe's hand.

"We're sure gonna see what he can do," Joe said.

"I know what he can do," said the cock sure Texan, with the Hoss Cartwright hat.

"Riders up!" was called. The jock's were legged up onto their prospective horses. And were now being led out to the pony people that would take them through the post parade, and on to the starting gate.

As Bobstoy was led out onto the race track, Joe looked over at the tote board. His horse had already been bet down to the odds of two-to-one. "Damn it," he said to himself. Looking again he saw that Amanda's horse was now at fifteen to one. This isn't good, Joe thought.

Amanda had also looked to see what the odds were. This was going to be something she had only heard about, and that was a boat race.

Charlie and Brian were pulling into the parking lot of Texas Downs.

"Charlie, looks like we're going to make the seventh race," Brian said as Charlie pulled into a parking space.

"Good, that was a wasted trip out there, I wonder where the little bastard went to?" Charlie said as they stepped from the pick-up.

"I don't know Charlie, but we better hurry, look, the horses are on the track."

The horses were now lined up and heading for the starting gate. Joe was watching as the gate hand took hold of Amanda's horse and loaded, the five horse went. It was now his turn. Once in the gate, he looked to his left, what he saw was Amanda looking back at him. She smiled and gave a short nod...he did the same. "Got one back!" Joe heard the gate hand say...

Up in the grandstand, Lisa Marie and her mother watched nervously at the monitor. Charlie and Brian had just walked up to the lady's.

"They're all in line...The announcer said, "They're off and racing...That's Bobstoy with the early lead, with Hot Sauce in second, a length back, followed by Hesahero...

As they head into the clubhouse turn that's Bobstoy, who has clearly gotten loose on the front end..."

Amanda was tucked in on the rail as she watched Joe set a lightning pace, she was in sixth place, about nine lengths off the horse in front of her. Her mount was running easily.

"That's it, Amanda, nice and easy, just stay where you're at," Charlie said.

The announcer was in full swing. "Racing down the back side Bobstoy is still in front with Hot Sauce right there...they've run the half in forty four flat...can you believe it!" The announcer taking a breath,...and then, continuing on "Bobstoy is still in front with Hot Sauce running a game second...then it's two back to Hesahero, followed by B.Jsgame...They're into the far turn, it's still Bobstoy in front by a length and a quarter, Hesahero has moved up to second, with Hot Sauce starting to fade...they're at the three eighths pole, Bobstoy is still strong on the lead, Hesahero making his move...Here comes B.Jsgame as he challenges Hesahero,...They're coming out of the turn, and down the stretch they come...Bobstoy still in front...but from way back, that's Imajet and Amanda Davis, as she guns down the leaders on the extreme outside. She quickly puts B.Jsgame away…and on to Bobstoy as he gives way to Imajet with less than seventy yards to go, it's all I'majet at the wire, clearly the winner, that's Bobstoy in for second, followed by B.Jsgame…"

In the Grandstand Lisa Marie touched Charlie's arm and asked. "Whadaya think?"

"It was believable, even though the pace was so fast," Charlie replied.

Having pulled her horse up, even though it had been a boat race, it sure felt good to win. That was her thought as she headed back to the winners circle.

As for Joe, this was the hard part. He hated going back to the trainers, trying to make excuses for something he had done on purpose.

Robert Jenson, the trainer of the horse Joe had just ridden, was waiting on Joe as he jogged up for the unsaddling. Joe's thought was, this ain't gonna be fun. Dismounting from Bobstoy, "Mr. Jenson, I'm sorry…"

He didn't get a chance to finish. "Sorry hell, son, I saw how you was trying to hold him back, I just had him to fresh. No, Joe, you rode a good race, don't worry, we'll get 'em next time."

"Yes, sir, Mr. Jenson. Thank you," Joe told the trainer.

"And by the way, Joe, send your agent by in the morning if you would."

"Sure thing," Joe said as he started back to the jock's room to get ready for the next race.

Walking into the room he was met by Amanda Davis. "Joe, thank you."

"Wait on me in the grandstand after you shower," Joe told her as he kept walking.

Meanwhile, Bradly had come to the point that he could tell that the big lights belonged to a race track. His biggest trouble now was who could he trust.

At another location where the R.V. had been moved to, Maggie was telling Lanette, "Well, we at least know they didn't catch Bradly."

"How do you know that?" Lanette asked.

"Well for one thing, I don't believe that they would have moved us unless they were afraid that Bradly would get help and come and find us."

"Yeah, I imagine you're right about that," Lanette said.

"You know what, sweetheart, I think that Bradly's safe and he's got help. At least he'll know to tell them we're in a big R.V. camper," Maggie said, and with that the two women fell silent, each to their own thoughts.

They hadn't had time to talk about what went on out at the rest area, during the seventh race. However, Lisa Marie had questions now. "So Charlie, did Billy ever come back to his car?"

"No, he didn't, I don't know what to make of it either. Kinda looks like he's doin' somethin funny. I'm definitely asking him some questions in the morning."

"Well, we've got one more to win, and then we can start on the next crazy ass thing the Headless Horseman wants us to do," Lisa Marie said, her voice full of contempt.

"Joe should win ths next one easily enough, at least I would think so," Charlie said.

"We'll find out soon enough," Tracy told the others.

Adding to the consensus, Brian said, "I'll have to agree with Charlie, out of everything Joe's ridden tonight, this is probably the best shot he has."

The horses were coming on to the track for the running of the eighth race. Joe and his mount "Shomethemoney," had drawn the number five hole, in against eight other rivals.

As Shomethemoney and Joseph were led by the tote board, he glanced over and saw that his odds were two-to-one. He smiled as he said, to the pony girl, "Let's warm up the winner."

"You're the boss, Jock," she replied as they started off in a jog.

Amanda had finished dressing and was now walking into the grandstand of Texas Downs. She herself looked at the odds board and saw that Shomethemoney was now at even money. Amanda took the escalator to the second floor, upon stepping off, she saw Charlie and Lisa Marie standing, there also was Joe's agent, Brian. Walking over to them, Lisa was the first to speak. "Amanda, you were so great out there tonight, you rode two very nice races."

"Thank you, Lisa, but I'm afraid we all know who did the work."

"It was a team effort, that went real well for the home team" said Charlie.

"So this is Amanda. Hi, I'm Lisa Marie's mother…"

Cutting in Lisa said, "I'm sorry, Mom, Amanda this is my mother, Tracy Gunn, Mom, meet Amanda Davis."

"Ladies and gentleman, the horses have reached the starting gate for the running of the eighth race this evening," the track announcer said.

Joseph and Shomethemoney were next to load, they were waiting on the number four horse to enter the gate. Joe happened to look over to the apron of the grandstand and he couldn't believe what he was seeing, or more to the point…who. "Bradly!"

"Dad!"

"One back, boss!" One of the assistant starters said.

"Locked up!" Another one said.

Time was going to fast for Joe to keep up, his brain just couldn't compute what was happening!

Back in the grandstand, the home team as Charlie had called them were glued to the television monitor.

"They're off and racing!" The announcer barked into the microphone. "That's Tap Dancing with the early lead…Wolf Pack is right there in second…As they enter the club house turn it's still Tap Dancing in front…it's a half length back to Wolf Pack followed by Imtheone, another two and half back to Shomethemoney…"

Joe had his mount tucked in on the rail as he entered the turn, just behind the leaders. Shomethemoney, had switched to his left, and was running with a relaxed long stride. Joe himself was comfortable and confident in the way that the race itself was unfolding, as they started down the backside.

Tap Dancer still has the lead by two,...that's Imtheone, now in second...followed by Wolf Pack, it's another three and a half back to Showmethemoney, they went the first half in forty five and two.

In the grandstand, Charlie was saying, "He's right where he needs to be. Now easy does it, Tee Joe."

Imtheone, has moved up to challenge Tap Dancer...Wolf Pack is right there..." The announcer was building a good stretch call. "Thats Mercedeswon up along side Shomethemoney...

Going into the far turn Imtheone, has taken a short lead, Tap Dancer still right there...Wolf Pack is running gamely in third, that's Shomethemoney on the move, with less than three eighths of a mile to go, they're bunched up nicely...Rope the Wind has gotten into the game as he starts his bid.

"Come on, Joe, start your move, you gotta go now, son," Charlie said, more or less under his breath.

The track announcer was getting excited as he continued calling the race, Imtheone has opened a two length lead...Wolf Pack had now taken over in second, up beside Wolf Pack on the outside that's Shomethemoney...and down the stretch they come!!!!!

That's Ropethewind on the extreme outside making a tremendous move as he blows by Shomethemoney...Shomethemoney, desperately trying to keep up..."

"Damn it; where did he come from?" Joe thought to himself as he switched to a left handed stick trying to get his horse to respond. And then it happened...The rider of Rope the Wind, switched to a right handed whip and whether his mount ducked from that or something on the outside fence, doesn't matter. The fact remains that Ropethewind, ducked in front of Shomethemoney, causing him to stumble.

"Hey, Hey, Hey,!!!!" Joe shouted to Ropethewinds jockey, but it was to late. The damage had already been done. Joe stood up in the irons, jerking up frantically, trying to keep Shomethemoney on his feet...

In the grandstand, Lisa Marie's heart skipped a beat as she watched her husband almost go down.

"Stumbling badly, is Shomethemoney,.Imtheone and Ropethewind are head and head as they race toward the wire...Wolf Pack is right there also...Here comes Shomethemoney, trying to vindicate himself as he runs past Wolf Pack..."

Lisa Marie was shouting. "Get up, Joe, damn it, get up!"

Charlie and the rest were all urging Joe to the front, "Get up, c'mon, Joe!"

With less than seventy yards to go it's all Imtheone, with Shomethemoney closing quickly...it's still Ropethewind, Shomethemoney right there, they're at the wire...it's...Ropethewind by a head, followed by Shomethemoney, next is Wolf Pack finishing third.

"Oh, Jesus, this isn't happening," Lisa Marie said.

At that very moment the infamous cell phone rang. With shaking hands, fumbling for it, Lisa Marie said as she looked at Charlie with pleading eyes, "Hello?"

"We played the game, and you knew the stakes," the voice of the Headless Horseman said.

"Wait, please don't..."

"Lisa!" Amanda said as she pointed to the two numbers flashing on the tote board.

"Ladies and gentleman, please hold all mutual tickets, there has been a stewards inquiry, along with a claim of foul by jockey Joseph Leblanc against the rider of the number six horse Felix Ortiz! Again, please hold all tickets!"

"Well, well, Lisa Marie, you just may have gotten lucky. I'll call back when the race has been declared official...

The phone call had ended.

"Thank you, dear Jesus," Lisa said aloud.

When Joe and Felix had pulled their mounts up in the middle of the turn. Joe indicated to the outrider to get on the radio, that he was lodging a claim of foul. And then to Felix, he said, "If they don't take your number down, I'm whipin' your ass, when we get back to the room!" And then he remembered seeing Bradly, Jesus he thought as he galloped back toward the winners circle.

In the grandstand, the announcer began. "Please let me have your attention, after reviewing the stretch run of the eighth race, the Stewards have determined that the number six impeded the running of the number five horse, the rider of Ropethewind did not maintain a straight course resulting in the disqualification of the six horse. The official order of finish has now been posted.

After the win picture was taken, Joseph weighed in and then was desperately looking for Bradly on the apron of the grandstand, but everywhere he looked there was no Bradly.

"Lisa Marie looking down to where her husband was, knew that something was wrong. "C'mom, quick! Joseph see's something down there!" They got to where Joe was at, about half way back to the jock's room. "Joseph, what's wrong?" Lisa Marie said.

"I saw Bradly! It was just before the race."

"Are you sure?" Charlie asked obviously excited.

"Everybody spread out," Lisa Marie said as she took a recent picture of Bradly from her purse. "Here Amanda, this is a picture of Bradly." Then taking another from her purse she started to hand it to Brian.

"I know what he looks like," Brian replied.

"Great, let's go," Lisa said, and then added, "Get changed, Joseph, and hurry."

Joe was already gone, and so was everyone else as they fanned out.

Little did they know that Bradly had met a man that he could trust and was now at the McDonald's, tearing into a hamburger and drinking a coke. He couldn't believe just how hungry he had been.

"So Bradly, do you think you could take me to where the R.V. was at."

"I'm sure I could," he said, between mouthfuls of burger and fries.

"Just take your time, Bradly, this time tomorrow you'll be back with your mom and dad."

"Damn it all to hell," said the Headless Horseman, when he had seen the man scoop up Bradly and hurry him out of the grandstand. He had been watching Brad, and waiting for just the right time to grab him. But now that was blown all to hell.

In the grandstand, they had searched everywhere, but no Bradly anywhere. Joseph had caught up with his wife and father.

"Joe, are you sure you saw Bradly?" Lisa Marie asked.

"I'm pretty sure that I'd know my own son, wouldn't you think?"

"I'm sure you would, it's just, where is he now?" Charlie said.

"I don't know, Dad, I just don't know," Joseph told his father.

Tears were starting to run down Lisa Marie's face as she began crying. "I don't know how much more of this I can take," she said.

Moving closer to his wife, he took her in his arms. "Lisa, it's going to be alright. I saw Bradly. We at least know he's alive."

"God, I hope so, Joseph," she told her husband.

Tracy and Brian along with Amanda were just walking up.

Did y'all have any luck?" Tracy asked.

"Not at all, Mom," Lisa Marie answered her mother as she began clearing her eyes.

"I don't understand where he could have went to," Joe told the others.

"Well, we know he's not here now. And besides Joe, isn't it possible that you made a mistake?" Brian asked.

"I just don't know, I thought I saw him, I guess it's possible, you know?" Joe replied.

"Well, why don't we go to the motel and get some rest? It's been a very long day for everyone," Tracy suggested.

"Sounds like a winner to me," Brian said.

Tracy and Brian, having said their goodnights, walked away.

"Amanda, I wanted to let you know just how grateful we are that you're helping us on this," Joseph told her.

"Joe, Lisa, I'm glad that I can help. I just wish that we would have met under different circumstances."

"C'mon y'all let's call it a night, I'm pretty damn wore out myself," Charlie told them.

The four of them then quietly walked from the grandstand.

Things were starting to come together. If this were actually a race, the announcer would be getting ready for the stretch call…and down the stretch they come!

Outside of the R.V. the Headless Horseman answered his cell phone. "Hello."

"Have you seen the boy?" the voice asked.

"Yeah, I saw him, I couldn't get him, though."

"Why not?"

"The guy with the F.B.I. has him."

Inside the R.V. Maggie told Lanette, "Sh-sh, now listen," she whispered. "He's on the phone, something about the F.B.I."

Outside again the man was saying, "So what do you want me to do now?"

"I'm not sure, I'll call back…" The line went dead.

The man that said he would call back turned to the boss and said, "The F.B.I. has the kid."

"Damn it, now we have to move the play up. I was having fun. Oh well, you know what to do."

"Are you sure this is what you want?" he asked.

"Yes," was the answer.

In the Leblanc's motel room, Joseph was pacing the floor and saying. "Why doesn't he call? He should have called by now."

"Take it easy, Joe, he'll call," Charlie told his son.

Lisa Marie walking out of the bathroom, looked very tired. Her eyes were swollen, the whole scenario had taken it's toll. Taking his wife in his arms he told her. "I love you Lisa, I promise we'll get them back."

"Joseph, you can't promise that, and we both know it…"

At that moment the phone rang. "There he is, Joseph," Charlie said.

Answering, he said, "Hello."

"Hello, Joe, well you did good tonight, it's a shame that it's almost over. However, you did win another chip, and for that you get a little treat. Now listen real close and don't say a word. I want you to get into the taxi that is now pullin up in front of your room. Tell your wife and father this is something you must do by yourself. If you don't, I will. If you're followed, the game will be over. Tick-Tick, times running…"

The call was disconnected. Joseph turning to face his wife and father he said, "I gotta go, he said I have to do this by myself, and don't follow me."

"Joseph, you can't!" Lisa Marie said.

"I have to!" Joe told her as he kissed her and said, "I love you always."

"I love you, too, Joseph, please be careful," she told him.

"Son, I love you, too, and like she said, be careful," Charlie said as he stood to give his son a hug.

The honking of the taxi startled each of them as Joe pulled away from his father, and then through the door he went.

Getting into the taxi, Joseph said, "I presume you know where to go."

"I do," the taxi driver replied.

Back in the motel room, Lisa Marie asked Charlie. "What do you make of this?"

"Lisa Marie, I wish I knew, but I don't."

"Do you think we should call Agent Pearce?" she asked.

"No, I think we should stay right here and wait," he answered as the cell phone rang again.

Lisa looked at Charlie as if to say, *What do I do.*

"Well, answer it!" Charlie said.

"Hello."

"Why, hello, Lisa Marie. Stay where you are, I'll call you back."

"What did he say?" Charlie asked, as Lisa Marie sat the phone down.

"Stay here until he calls back," she replied.

Meanwhile David Pearce had called in two more agents. One was now with young Bradly, the other was watching the room where Lisa Marie and Charlie were at. He was still trying to get it all straight in his mind as to what happened to Gerard Fontenot all those years ago, and what was happening now.

The convenience store clerk that had waited on Gerard, had actually come through with a very old secret that had been since the night Fontenot had been killed.

Then some other help had come in the form of a faxed picture from a friend with the Louisiana Racing Board, which had been faxed to another person, who confirmed it. As he was thinking of all this, his cell phone beeped…Answering it. "Hello," he said.

"It's me Pearce, Jackson. The taxi took Leblanc to the High Sierra Motel off of interstate ten, it's about five miles west of where you are."

"Did he go into a room?" Pearce asked.

"Yeah, the taxi dropped him off and then left, Leblanc knocked on room one fifty six, somebody opened the door. And he went in."

"Could you see who opened it?"

"No, I sure didn't," Jackson replied.

"Okay, I want you to stay right there, if anything changes, you call me pronto, got it?"

"I got it," Jackson said.

After the call had ended Pearce sat there in his car wondering just who could have been waiting in the room for Joseph. Was Joe Leblanc, a part of this whole thing. As he thought about it, his mind went back to tonights races, between him and Amanda Davis they had won some races with good payoffs, plus the pick three which by itself on a two dollar ticket had paid seventy five hundred. Pearce picked his phone up, punched in a number and waited… "Hello," a voice said.

"Jackson, go to the front desk and see who's name that room is in, then call me back."

"Gotcha, boss."

No sooner had that call ended than another rang. "Hello," Pearce answered.

"Yeah, look Pearce, this is Anderson, we have the G.P.S. (Global positioning system) on the R.V., you were right on the money with the owners name."

"That's great Anderson, so now you can track it," Pearce said.

"Sure can, as a matter of fact, we're in route right now via helicopter, here's the address...

After getting the location of the R.V. he ended the call. The phone beckoned to be answered right away. "Hello."

"It's me again, Jackson..."

"You're not going to believe this..."

Pearce was now heading to the location of the R.V. shaking his head and saying aloud to himself. "Well, I'll be damned, talk about switching things up."

Arriving just down the street from the R.V. Pearce using his radio, contacted the helicopter. "I'm in position, how do you want to handle this?"

"Pearce, there's two agents on the backside of the R.V. they have a visual on our target, a special operations officer is going to the door. I want you to stand down on this one."

"Ten four, I copy that," Pearce replied with some relief.

At that very moment the special operations officer knocked on the door to the R.V. "Who is it?" the man on the inside asked.

"Grandmom, wake up," Lanette whispered.

"What is it, baby?" Maggie asked.

"Somebody just knocked on the door."

"Who is it?" the man asked again.

"Yeah, sorry to bother you all, but I just live down the street here, and I can't find my dog."

"You mean to tell me," the man said as he threw the door open, "this is about some damn dog?" He also had his gun in hand. That's when one of the agents, shot him in the back. He wasn't dead, the three operatives then rushed the R.V. What they found was two very scared Leblanc's.

Pearce being called on the radio again. "Pearce, I want this place cleared quickly! We want it to be as if nothing took place here, hopefully the other members will show up here.

"Mrs. Leblanc, my name is David Pearce, I know that you have been through quite an ordeal. Very soon now, you'll be with your family, you too, Lanette."

Clearing the area, and placing agents in and around the R.V., Pearce then took Maggie and Lanette to the motel, his intention was to unite the family. However, upon arriving, he found their room empty. Where in the hell could they have gone, he asked himself. That's when his phone rang. Answering. "Hello!"

"It's Jackson again, what's going on?"

"What in the hell, do you mean by that!" Pearce snapped.

"Well, Charlie and Lisa Marie Leblanc just pulled up."

"Don't do anything, I'm on my way!!" After placing Maggie and Lanette in the protection of the agent that already had Bradly, he took off for the High Sierra Motel

"Charlie, what do you thinks going on in there?" Lisa Marie asked.

"Lisa, I don't know, I really don't," Charlie replied.

"Well, let's go find out, whadaya say?" Lisa said.

"Let's go," he agreed.

Walking up to the room that the Headless Horseman had told them to, when he had called back, seconds before he had been shot.

"Go ahead and knock, Charlie," Lisa Marie told him, which he did. "Who is it?" A woman's voice asked.

"It's Charlie Leblanc," he said, and then he heard from the other side of the door. "God damn it, how did they know we were here."

"Charlie, I know that voice," Lisa Marie said.

"Open this damn door!" Charlie shouted.

When it did open, they got something they never expected. "What in the god damned hell, is going on here?" Lisa Marie said as she barged into the room. Standing there in nothing but a skimpy tee shirt was Amanda Davis. Joseph Leblanc lay there in bed, covered only in a sheet, and appeared to be just waking up. "Joe Leblanc, you sorry son of a bitch," Lisa Marie yelled at her husband. That's when Agent Pearce and Agent Jackson burst into the room.

"Everybody freeze, I would have never in a million years thought this," Pearce said.

"I'll second that," Charlie said as he shook his head.

"Joseph Greaden Leblanc, you're under arrest for race fixing, racketeering, fraud, and whatever else I can think of."

Agent David Pearce said these things as Lisa Marie walked from the room.

"Would somebody, please tell me what in the hell happened?" Joe asked, looking very confused.

"Mr. Leblanc, please get dressed," Agent Jackson said, while Pearce went outside to talk with Lisa Marie, Charlie also walked out on his son.

"Mrs. Leblanc, I do have some good news for you. Your son and daughter, along with your wife, Mr. Leblanc, well they're at the motel."

"Are you sure Mr. Pearce?" Charlie asked.

With tears in her eyes, Lisa Marie said, "Please, Charlie, let's go."

"Lisa, go ahead and get in the truck, I need to talk with Pearce here for a minute. I'll be right there."

"Okay, Charlie, please hurry, though. I want to get to my babies."

Agent Jackson was bringing Joseph out in handcuffs as Charlie finished his talk with Pearce. "Dad, I got set up. Please tell Lisa Marie!"

"Joseph, I don't know what to believe, we might talk later, but for now, I'm going to see my wife." He then turned and walked away.

Turning around he looked pleadingly at Amanda Davis. "What happened, Amanda?" he asked. She only smiled as she closed the door.

"You should be arresting that bitch, not me!" Joseph told them.

"C'mon, Leblanc, let's go," Pearce said.

On the way to the motel Charlie said, "Lisa, maybe what we saw back there isn't what the real deal is. I judged that boy to quick once.

I just hope I'm not doing the same thing now." For the rest of the ride, each were lost in their own thoughts.

Meanwhile, parked down the street with his lights off, the second member of the Headless Horseman group got out of his car. He carried a gallon of gasoline. His mind was made up on what he was about to do.

However, he didn't realize that every step he took, he was being watched.

In another place, a phone call was being received. "Hello," the voice said.

"Hi, it's Amanda. It's done."

"Good, he'll be by in about thirty minutes, you know what to do."

"Yes, I know." Then the line went dead.

After the F.B.I. had left, she had gotten dressed and went to another motel, where the room was in someone elsies, name. She was now relaxing and also thinking about the money she was earning. She smiled and said, "How sweet it is."

Lisa Marie was now hugging her children as tears of joy fell. Charlie also was hugging his wife, when she suddenly pulled back and asked, "Where's Joseph?"

Charlie didn't know what to say to his wife… "Charlie, where's my son?"

"Maggie, he's done some things, that well, they put him in jail for, but we'll know a little more about it in the morning," Charlie told his wife.

"In the morning, we're going to go get him out of there and I don't give one red damn cent about how much it cost, are we clear on that?"

"Baby, in the morning, we'll be a lot more informed," Charlie told her.

Everyone was so tired and exhausted that the kids crawled in the bed and were fast asleep

"So, Mr. Pearce, the Headless Horseman was actually that little bastard Ronnie Deville that Joe whipped the hell out of. He always was a trouble maker," Charlie said.

"Yeah, Mr. Leblanc that was him alright. I'll be able to explain a lot better in the morning. What y'all need is a goodnights rest. We'll talk in the morning," Agent Pearce told him. And then he said his goodnights. Although, this night was for from being over.

The F.B.I. had their eyes trained on the man with the gallon of gasoline.

"Bear in the woods," the agent said as he keyed the mike on his radio.

"Hold steady, and stand down, let him roll, we'll follow; do you copy?"

"Ten four, we copy, I need four copies, let's hear 'em."

"Copy one."

"Copy two."

"Copy three."

"Copy four."

So they only watched as the man crawled under the R.V., he took what looked to be a tee shirt, which he pushed one end of it into the gallon of gas, the other end, he lit with a lighter, then quickly he crawled out and was running to his car. Reaching it, he didn't wait for the fireworks, he figured he could read about it later. As he pulled on to Interstate ten, headed to see Amanda, he had no idea that a whole bunch of F.B.I. agents were following him.

Pulling into her motel, he stopped in front of room one twenty seven, he got out of his car with a satchel.

After one sharp knock, the door was opened, he stepped in.

"So it looks like you got your part done," the man said.

"It went real smooth, Lisa Marie really thought we had been in bed," she laughed, as she said this.

"Yeah, I would like to have seen that," he said.

"Look, lay the money on the bed, I've got a little something I want you to have." As she said this, Amanda moved toward the bathroom and then she turned toward the man, this time though, she was holding a three fifty seven with a silencer on it. "There's been a little change in plans…" she said.

At that moment, the door flew open. "Everybody freeze, F.B.I. …M'am, put the gun down, now!" Even Amanda Davis knew when to quit.

In the Leblancs motel room, Lisa Marie lay in bed with her children, they were asleep, she wasn't. Something kept bugging her about the whole thing, something was all wrong. But what was it, then like lightning it hit her, she jumped out of bed, and throwing a robe on she left the room, knocking on her mothers room, the door opened but before her mother actually saw her she said, "Well, it's about damn time."

"Who were you expecting mother," Lisa Marie said.

Recovering quickly she said, "Oh, I thought you were Brian."

"And just where is Brian, Mom? Oh, never mind, what I want to know is, how did you know that Joe didn't have to win one of those races tonight? You remember, your exact words were…It's a good thing that he doesn't have to win this one. What did you mean by that?"

Walking up to the room, the door still open, agent David Pearce said, "Maybe I can help with that, Mrs. Leblanc."

Charlie Leblanc had gotten dressed and was now outside as well. "What's goin on here?" Charlie asked.

"Well, for starters, Mrs.Gunn, you are under arrest for racketeering, extortion, conspiracy to commit murder as well as kidnaping," Pearce stated.

"You're crazy, that's the craziest thing I've ever heard," Tracy said as she lit a cigarette.

"No, Mrs. Gunn, it's not, and you and I both know it. Let me run it down to you."

"No, I want this pleasure," Joseph Leblanc said as he walked into the room, where everyone had gathered.

"Joseph!" Lisa Marie said.

"Lisa, I didn't sleep with Amanda, I was given rompum, you know, horse tranquilizer, xilazine. Don't look so surprised Tracy, you ordered it. You see, this is what happened. Gerard your father, Lisa, was a good man. Your mom here was having an affair with Brian. Your father didn't know it though. He had been approached by Brian to throw the stake race at Vinton that night. He wouldn't do it though. So while he slept that night after being drugged, Brian came in the room and together your mom and Brian got him up, mine you the drugs were really kicking his ass, but they finally steered him to the car."

"This is all fricken lies, you little bastard!" Tracy shouted.

"No, it's the truth, you're an evil ass woman. It was Brian that went into that store that night, not Gerard. The mistake he made was buying cigarettes, Gerard didn't smoke. And it was Brian that killed your father, but your mother was the one that planned it. You see, what no one else knew was that she had taken out a life insurance policy on Gerard. She collected over one hundred thousand dollars. That was an awful lot of money in nineteen seventy two."

The air had been sucked from her she felt so weak she could no longer stand, Joseph rushed to his wife, as her knees buckled. "Joe," she said.

"It's okay, I'm here for you," he told her.

"That's the god damned trouble!" Tracy shouted, as she pulled a snub nose thirty eight from her purse. She should not have done that. David Pearce in a flash had raised his 9 mm and said,"don't!" It was to late, she had leveled it at Joseph. Agent Pearce shot her through the heart.

Three months later sitting at the kitchen table of their new home in Carrencro, Louisiana, Lisa Marie told her husband. "I'm so sorry that I doubted you that night."

"It's over, we don't ever have to mention it again."

"I love you, Joe."

"I love you, too."

Tracy Gunn died that night, she was buried in the Lafayette Cemetery. Her husband Brian is now serving two consecutive life sentences for murder, kidnaping, and conspiracy to commit murder.

The first member of the Headless Horseman also died from complications while they removed the bullet that was lodged in his chest. Amanda Davis was sentenced to a mandatory ten years in Prison. Joseph Leblanc was never brought to trial. He now rides races where it all began…Cajun Downs.

Printed in the United States
57929LVS00002B/188